# "I Dreamed I Loved Someone Once.

"Then my dream slowly shredded away to nothing," Ann explained.

Clint saw her disillusionment and said gently, "That's why we're waiting. I want you to be sure."

"I'm afraid."

"Do you realize that you love me, Ann?" Clint asked.

"I resist knowing. You're too disruptive. I'm uneasy."

"But not afraid?" he probed.

She answered, "That, too. Not of you, but for my peace."

"You can't live in a cocoon, wrapped snugly away from living."

"But I have my paintings and my backyard and my cat," she countered.

"No people?"

"My sister is my contact."

"Not I?"

Earnestly she told him, "I'm so tempted with you. But it's as if I must leap from the cliff into fog. I don't know where I'll land."

He moved his hand to touch the side of her head. "I would be there to catch you, to lead you through the fog and guide your steps until you can see."

Dear Reader:

Welcome to Silhouette! What better way to celebrate St. Valentine's Day and all the romance that goes with it than to indulge yourself with a Silhouette Desire?

If this is your first Desire, let me extend an invitation for you to sit back, kick off your shoes and enjoy. If you are a regular reader, you already know what awaits you.

A Silhouette Desire can encompass many varying moods and tones. The books can be deeply emotional and dramatic, or charming and lighthearted. But no matter what, each and every one is a sensual, compelling love story written by and for today's women.

I know you'll enjoy February's *Man of the Month*, *A Loving Spirit* by Annette Broadrick. But I think *all* of the February books are terrific. Give in to Desire . . . you'll be glad you did!

All the best,

Lucia Macro
Senior Editor

# LASS SMALL
## CONTACT

SILHOUETTE *Desire*

Published by Silhouette Books New York

**America's Publisher of Contemporary Romance**

SILHOUETTE BOOKS
300 East 42nd St., New York, N.Y. 10017

ISBN: 0-373-05548-X

First Silhouette Books printing February 1990

Printed in the U.S.A.

## LASS SMALL

finds that living on this planet at this time is a fascinating experience. People are amazing. She thinks that to be a teller of tales of people, places and things is absolutely marvelous.

This is my twenty-fifth published book—
a milestone.
Therefore I would like to salute
all those who have read my books.
And special regards to all those
who have written to my editors and to me.
Thank you.

# One

The reclusive Ann Forbes lived in a house in the Broad Ripple section of Indianapolis. She was an artist, and the interior of the house had been altered to suit her needs. On that particular day in June, Ann and her sister were in the combined living and dining rooms, which Ann had converted into her studio.

Seated at her tilted drawing table, the dark-haired Ann protested, "But I *don't* want to go!" She was uncharacteristically strident. She even looked up from her drawing to frown at her very blonde sister standing in the middle of the cluttered room.

"You have to." Mary was so positive that her fists were clenched. Her sister hadn't been to any gathering in—how long? Mary was determined as she pushed: "I can't find anyone else. You owe me. If it weren't for me, you wouldn't be here. Mom and Dad had me in order not to be childless and—"

"I know. I know. And they had me so you wouldn't be an only child."

"See? It was for *me*! You are here for my convenience. So you have to go. I'd rather take Fiona. She isn't a dog, but she's no competition. She can't go, and I don't want to be there alone, so you must go with me." Mary paused, then felt the need to add, "You're no competition either, but men don't realize right away that you're not interested."

Mildly Ann continued in the negative: "There is nothing on earth more boring than corporate cocktail parties."

"They are the prime hunting ground for women to find power men," declared the divorced Mary. "I'm not going to live in a cottage with a white picket fence. You *have* to go with me because this is special. Besides the usual attendees, we have the five big men who are moving to Indianapolis, and they'll be there. At least three will be married, but at this age and echelon, two should be divorced, and I should be able to attract one."

Ann looked up at Mary and closed her right eye. She had a new contact lens in her left eye. It was so unusual to see through that eye so clearly that it fascinated her. Distracted, she asked her sister, "Is money all you want out of life?"

Mary waved her arms to widen such a simple premise. "Position. Power. *And* lots of money."

"It's definitely overrated." Ann was positive.

"Harry was a fluke." Mary gave her sister a careful look. She knew that Ann's ex-husband had left scars. Harry Warsaw was now about forty years old and had his own manufacturing corporation, which was headquartered in Indianapolis.

"He had money and looks. He appeared to have it all." Ann went back to drawing.

Mary knew only that Harry had verbally abused his young wife to such an extent that it had changed Ann's personality. She told her sister, "He fooled everyone. He still does. He's the rule-proving exception. Real power men are superior men. They are more intelligent, they know how to delegate authority, and they are efficient. When they play, they use the scope of those same talents and commitments."

In gentle teasing, Ann guessed, "You've been reading *Fortune* again."

"The very title fascinates me." Mary's movements were easier as the tone of their exchange lightened. "This place is a mess."

"Close your eyes."

"There are times, Ann, when I'm not at all sure our parents actually had you. Look how different we are. Night and day. Brunette and blond; black eyes and blue eyes. We simply don't match. Twenty-six years ago, at one and a half, I wasn't old enough to verify the authenticity of your birth. I suspect that some remarkable woman exchanged you for the ordinary child who is really my sister. You're a changeling. Or there's always the real possibility that our parents could have found you under a bush and passed you off as one of us."

They exchanged a smile, for that was an old, old speculation in their family. Their parents claimed Ann was a hospital swap, because they'd never have been able to produce such a unique jewel.

"Say you'll go with me on Friday," Mary coaxed.

"I think you've already used up all the IOUs relating to my birth. You are now running on friendship. What have you done for me lately?"

"You still owe me for going and rescuing you from that obsolete hippie commune down in west Texas—" she paused for effect "—in *August*."

"I learned strength from them. I learned survival. I learned a lot out there."

"I just bet you did."

"All you think of is money and sex."

Mary lifted her hands and brows. "Tell me what's more important."

"Freedom." Ann was sure.

"That's what money represents."

"If you persist in chasing idiocy, I suppose I should monitor your attempts. I'll...go."

No one could sound more reluctant. Over her jubilance Mary heartlessly contrived a laugh. "Great. I knew you would." Then, to appear abrasively teasing so that Ann wouldn't suspect her, she declared, "I anticipated the entire resistance, but I knew you would have to give in and go." She continued the bantering directions: "Don't wear anything too weird or wild. *And quit checking out that contact!* You look strange with one eye closed half the time. Remember the party is Friday, at six, in the conference room. Since the receptionist will vanish at five, I'll give your name to Security in the lobby. Do you remember how to find the conference room?"

"Probably."

"*Probably?* Good solid reassurance there." Mary managed to glare at Ann. With great patience she made her instructions offhand. "You go to the fourteenth floor and go in the left door. Left. That's the contact eye. Walk down the hall until you come to a cross corridor. Turn right. The conference room is at the end of the hall. Got it?''

"It seems simple enough.''

After all her plotting, Mary almost blew it. She heard herself blurting, "You need a keeper. It's no wonder Harry tricked you into marrying him.'' Mary's words stopped. "That's nonsense. You know that. Harry fools everyone.''

"There are times when I believe I could become quite fond of you.''

Mary grinned. "Me, too. Remember. Don't wear anything stupid. And watch the colors. Be discreet.''

"I wish we'd had another sister. Someone to share the pressure, instead of just me.''

"I'll get you whipped into shape one of these years.''

"I wish to God you'd marry and have seven children in five years.''

"Revenge is tacky. Be there. At six on Friday. The conference room.''

"I really don't want to go." Ann tried to withdraw.

Feeling her plot crumbling, Mary flung her arms wide. "If there was *any* alternative, you wouldn't *need* to!''

"That ought to make you appreciate me.''

"I do—but with great caution.''

After Mary left, Ann tacked up three very large signs that read: Six Friday, Conference Room. One was on the refrigerator, one on the bathroom mirror, and one on the inside of the front door.

So on Friday Ann changed into a quieter dress— three times—before she settled on a cream silk that skimmed her body and was lovely. She put her long dark hair into a high, sleek knot on the back of her head, leaving a jaw-length strand before each ear. Using a bit more makeup than she ordinarily wore, she put pearls in her ears and draped a long strand around her throat. She slid her toes into slender, cream-colored, high-heeled slippers, then took up a Spanish shawl of creams and lightning blues with a long, creamy fringe.

Ann looked as she'd calculated: elegant, unapproachable, intimidating.

Going outside, she surveyed her dirty car. There wasn't any way at all that she dared put her cream dress inside that dusty vehicle, so she called a cab. Consequently she was late. Just off the Circle in downtown Indianapolis, she paid the cabbie, then hesitated before she made the final commitment and crossed the walk through the evening crowds. She went into the Art Nouveau-decorated lobby of the building where Mary was an accountant for an international law firm.

Ann rode the elevator to the fourteenth floor. The doors slid open to reveal Mary, who exclaimed in relief, "Come *on*! I didn't think you'd ever get here!"

"I had to take a cab. Rush hour. Sorry."

"What happened to your car? Did you have to look that good? Well, it's too late now. Come on inside."

"Hello to you, too."

In a buffeting reassurance, Mary scolded, "When I told you to be elegant, I meant reasonably, not *this* good. Stand in a corner and be quiet. I don't need any amateur competition."

"Is it all right if I eat?" Ann inquired drolly.

"People never eat at cocktail parties."

"Why are you out here?"

"I didn't know anyone I wanted to walk in with. I'm basically insecure."

Ann laughed in pure delight as Mary took her arm and tugged her along the posh corridor. "Quit laughing. It makes you very animated and attractive. Look glum."

"How's this?" Ann sobered.

"You disgust me. Now you look as if you know a delicious joke. Why can't you just be vacant and uninteresting?"

"I was found under a bush."

"That leads to all sorts of speculation as to who your parents really are."

"Gypsies. I realized it long ago."

"Of course. That would explain the fascination with the commune. Here we are. Be quite. Stand in a corner and play dead."

"Right away?"

"Okay, you can say hello to Mr. Byford. He's the office manager, if you will recall. Don't be too friendly. He takes 'friendly' very seriously. A cool nod is best."

"And food," Ann insisted. "I'll bet Sharon catered this spread and you know how delicious the goodies are."

"Then eat! My God, why don't you weigh three hundred pounds?"

"It's my gypsy heritage. It comes genetically from centuries of having to run to avoid apprehension. Therefore we have lean genes."

"Oh, quiet. Leave the men alone."

"Check."

"Ah, Mr. Byford. You remember my sister, Ann?"

"Well, hel-lo!" Mr. Byford was edging into fifty, and having worked furiously all his life, he was now looking around and realizing he'd been missing a great deal. He wanted it all—and right away.

Ann lifted a cool nose and said levelly, "Mr. Byford," then walked on past with no hesitation. She eased herself through the press of bodies to the table of hors d'oeuvres. There she selected a plateful of flaky crusts holding crab and shrimp, and puffs stuffed with ham or chicken. Carrying the goodies, she automatically went to stand by the far wall to avoid contact with any of the other guests. She began to sample Sharon's genius with exquisite hedonistic relish. That meant she had to allow her taste buds sufficient time to savor each bite, which gave her eyes idle time.

Her sister was a blond shaft of light that flickered and glowed with vitality and charm. As Mary laughed and sparkled, Ann smiled softly and took another bite. She discreetly cleared her lips with her tongue, and her eyelids narrowed as she considered the subtle flavor.

After she'd finished thoroughly tasting the bit and had swallowed, she looked indolently around the room, resting her palate. Closing her right eye, she viewed the gathering through the new, remarkable contact lens. She noted there were many more men than women. This was a man's world, and the men exuded power. The magnetism of the group could probably be measured on sensors. These men were movers and shapers. They moved events and people their way and shaped the results to suit their needs. Most people found such an atmosphere stimulating and exciting. Her ex-husband had cured Ann of that.

Examining the plate to choose the next experience, Ann carefully licked her lips and almost smiled in anticipation. She lifted the bit to her mouth, and as she rolled it on her tongue to give it full scope, she closed her eyes in order to concentrate properly. Delicious!

She opened almost sated eyes to gaze here or there. There were several men vying for her sister's attention, and Mary was handling them all with ease. Most of the males were there for a purpose—to be seen or to make contact. They were impressive. Interested glances studied Ann, but she looked away indifferently, not encouraging any approach. Gazes still came her way. She looked again at her plate.

With another taste, her glance rested on a single figure who stood across the crowded room. That he was alone was different. In his midthirties, he stood strongly, his feet apart, his suit jacket unbuttoned, one hand in a trouser pocket, the other holding a drink. He made an interesting contrast to the pattern of the other bodies.

Closing her right eye, Ann surveyed him—aesthetically—through her contact. He was worth the effort, for he was beautifully male. As an artist, she moved her appreciating left eye up his fine body with pleasure. Very male. His trousers could not conceal the fact. His belt showed a flat middle and his chest told that he did more than sit at a desk. His shoulders were his own: no padding. And his neck was that of an athlete—strong, hard and sloping into his wide shoulders. A football player? His dark head was held high . . . and his blue eyes were looking straight into hers.

Ann opened her right eye and stared, and he very slowly closed his left one in a deliberate wink.

She glanced aside, then back to him. He'd been flirting. A form approached him, to whom he gave minimal bits of attention and replies, his eyes only flicking briefly aside to the intruder before they came back to watch Ann.

She turned away and leaned her shoulder against the wall, pointedly dismissing the man. She looked at her plate and found only one last bit of tempting marvel. She picked it up and enjoyed a puff of deviled ham. Then, congratulating herself for not licking the plate, she went back to the table and selected another group of perfect nibbles.

As Ann completed her round of the table, she saw that the man was extricating himself from what was now a group who wanted to talk to him. His gaze came to her and he smiled a little. His intent was obvious: he planned to speak to her. To avoid him, she slid between some bodies, went to the serving door and told a harried Sharon, "If ever I should marry again, you shall do the catering. I can't afford you yet for my shows."

"When I can afford you, I want you to paint my son Greg."

"Set a time. We'll work out a trade."

"Would you . . . really?"

"I have a great appreciation of your talent."

Then Ann instantly realized that he was there. She felt his presence nearby. It was as if a powerful, disruptive force had intruded into her space. She resisted turning but watched as Sharon looked at him, and the smile Sharon sent beyond Ann was the kind women saved for a certain breed of men. Ann fought the need to escape.

His voice vibrated dangerously inside Ann as he said to Sharon, "You're the caterer? You've done a very fine table."

Sharon smiled helplessly and said a muffled "Thank you."

Tongue-tied? Sharon? Ann still didn't turn toward him. Instead she moved her head up and turned it away a little. Hoping for...escape? Yes.

Still speaking to Sharon, he said, "For your advertising video—and you should consider one—you should show this lady as she tastes your hors d'oeuvres. Watching her made me feel as if I've been starved all my life."

He wasn't talking about hors d'oeuvres. A shimmer almost like fear shivered through Ann. She was in danger. Her heart began to falter and her breathing was disturbed. She swallowed, straightened her spine, and flouting peril, she turned to dispel the foolish, imaginative silliness with a straight, practical stare. He could not be as formidable as she had conjured. In three-inch heels, her eyes were level with his stubborn chin. She lifted her stare to his face, and he was *exactly* as she'd feared. He smiled. My God. He was exactly so.

Where was Mary? Ann wondered why she had come there. She looked beyond him and saw the shaft of sunlight that was her sister, and she winked a quick signal for Mary to come save her.

He said, "I'm Clint Burrows."

Ann nodded, accepting that, her breathing shallow in her disquiet.

Sharon said, "May I give you a card? I cater any time, any type of gathering."

"Please." He said it nicely. "Our people already know you, but give me several to pass along."

Sharon handled it well. She didn't give him a whole fistful of cards, just a few. Then she went about her business, leaving Ann Forbes there alone in that crowded room with Clint Burrows. Ann again looked beyond him, caught Mary's eye and winked again quickly.

He ventured careful opening words. "I saw you come in with the blonde. Are you friends?"

"Sisters."

"Full sisters?" He was speaking in the calm, ordinary, almost conciliatory way of men who were being careful to find a way to talk to a woman and not scare her off. The only kind of men who knew to do that were the ones who realized how very dangerous they really were, and they knew smart women were skittish around them. He coaxed for a response. "You're quite unlike one another."

"They've figured I was really a gypsy child left under a bush."

He grinned, feeling he had a toehold. "So you dance?"

"No."

"Play a violin?"

"No."

She wasn't being very helpful. He said, "It just happens that I do play a violin. If I play for you, would you dance for me?"

"Only on street corners. And I get the quarters." It was an automatic reply used since she was almost fifteen. It sounded shudderingly adolescent.

"Deal." He put out his hand to shake on it, but she only looked at him. She knew better than to actually touch him.

He was a trial lawyer and part of his skill was in reading people. Without thinking he told her, "I'm harmless." He was serious, and he surprised himself.

She only watched him, unconvinced by such a foolish misstatement.

Mary came to where they were apparently rooted in the doorway of the serving kitchen. "Ann." She bubbled with laughter and self-confidence. "This is Dingus McGee. You can tell by his name that he's Italian," she teased, laughing up at the redheaded man beside her who was so amused. She told him, "This is my sister, Ann Forbes. And ... ?" She looked expectantly at the man who stood with Ann.

Ann said nothing, so Clint replied, "I'm Clint Burrows."

Dingus said, "My God. Clint Burrows? I didn't know you'd gotten here! Welcome to Indianapolis. You really give us clout. I thought you were a hundred feet tall!"

Clint smiled. "No. I hear good things about you."

"About me?" Dingus put his hand on his chest to identify which "me" he meant. "You've heard about me?"

"That you did an exceptional job for the Parkinsons."

"You heard about that?"

Clint was kind. "Yes."

Dingus was an honest man and disclaimed a false label of cleverness. "You know, all it really took was just time. The Parkinsons are such nice people. I had to do something."

"You found the solution." Clint understood Dingus and credited him. "It was well done."

"Thank you. That means more to me than I could ever tell you, just to hear Clint Burrows say that."

"You're welcome." He looked at Mary. "So you're the gypsy's sister."

"She told you about that?"

"I'm going to play the violin, and she's going to dance."

"Really?" Surprised and alert, Mary looked at Ann. "I want to be there."

Clint agreed to that. "You can pass the hat. She's claimed all the quarters."

Since adults in the legal field never actually did anything so foolish, Dingus decided to be a part of the frivolous nonsense. "I can play a Jew's harp."

Clint consulted with Ann. "Would a Jew's harp go all right with a violin?"

"Yes." She was sober, her eyes were serious, as if she looked down a corridor no one else could see.

"When?" Again he didn't seem to be talking about the subject but was beyond it to another meaning.

Mary asked, "Now?"

Dingus became cautious. "Here in Indianapolis?"

"Indianapolis is quite cosmopolitan," Mary promised. "I was walking down the street one noon, and a man in front of me, carrying laundry in a sheet, stopped and sorted through the clothes right on the sidewalk. We have our own eccentrics. We can pass for New York City or London any time."

"There's no violin." Ann lifted her chin coolly.

"Bart Byford just happens to have one in his office. He's a closet concert player. I'll borrow that."

With hasty relief, Dingus eliminated himself. "My harp's at home."

Clint smiled. "You can clap your hands and set the rhythm."

Mary laughed in a marvelous, amazed chuckle. "Done! Let's go."

Clint lifted amused brows at Dingus. "Game?"

"To the death!" He raised a clenched fist, committing himself, but he knew he was being brave and rash.

Clint looked then at Ann. "And you?"

"Of course." Ann knew she had just done something extremely reckless, something she would regret. This man was not an ordinary man. If she came close to him, it could be disastrous. That was what she saw down that invisible corridor—turmoil, emotion. She could be wrecked. Why didn't she shun this encounter? All she had to say was "How foolish" in a quelling way. She began, "How—"

And Mary exclaimed, "I can't believe this! How fun! Let's get the violin! Ann, you're human!"

Then Clint touched her. He took her arm in his strong fingers, and he said softly just to her, "Human? I thought you were a dream. You are real?"

"Disappointingly."

"Not so far."

"You are doomed to disillusion."

"Doomed, anyway."

Soberly they looked at each other—really saw each other—and realized exactly what was happening. It was a once-in-a-lifetime encounter; and in each one, there was not only the awareness of fate, but a feeling of great emotional turbulence.

As Bart came to their group, they heard Mary asking, "Mr. Byford, could Clint borrow your violin?"

Only that broke the gaze between the pair. Clint tore his eyes from Ann's and echoed Mary. "I'll take good care of it."

Bart asked cautiously, "Will you play it here?"

"No. We'll be on a street corner."

That went through the room like wildfire. "What?" "What's Clint up to?" "A what? A violin?" "...Did he say on a street corner?" Therefore, as they left there was a comet's tail of curious followers, questioning what was going on, where they were going, and why. "You're serious?" "Clint's mixed up in this?" "Yes." "Then I'll have to see this for myself."

They left the suite of offices and had to wait for those elevators designated to run after hours. They filtered from the building and walked to the Circle, that hub of Indianapolis. Since the area was cherished and used, it was jammed at night.

Ann was strangely calm. It was as if this had to happen, and she couldn't do anything to prevent it. She was committed beyond herself to seeing it through. It was as if she was in a time warp. It was her Kismet.

She walked beside Clint because he held her arm in his hand. His hand was hard and warm on that June night. In his other hand was the violin in its case. He walked with purpose, although he matched her slower pace, and he looked around in the aloof way of a man who knew where he was and who else was around him.

Dingus and Mary followed them. Mary was astounded and stimulated, while Dingus was somewhat surprised to find himself a party to this bizarre happening.

They stopped by the small church crowded next to the Columbia Club, and Dingus held out his arms for the violin case just as Mr. Byford came up. "I'll hold the case," he offered. It was a strange happening—one Bart Byford would never have joined. But anything Clint did changed the circumstances. Bart would go along with it, so long as they didn't take off their clothes and jump into the Circle's fountain. Had he been younger, he might even have gone along with that.

Clint tuned the violin, listening as he touched the strings, his gaze on Ann. He tightened the bowstrings while Dingus searched among the followers for a hat. They borrowed a passerby's who was intrigued with what was going on. He eyed the two women involved in whatever was coming off—one so blond and the other such a mysterious brunette—and he grinned.

With élan, Ann took off her shoes and handed them to Mary. She loosened her dark hair so that it tumbled around her shoulders, and she tied the shawl around her hips so the fringe almost touched the sidewalk. Then she stood and bowed her head in slow formal acknowledgement that she was ready to begin.

Looking at her reclusive sister, Mary said, "I'd never believe this if I weren't here."

Heartily agreeing with that, Dingus laughed with some nervousness. His family was really very formal.

Ann replied woodenly, "It's my fate."

Thinking Ann was renewing a long-submerged drollness, Mary grinned and darted a sharing look at her sister, but Ann's black eyes were watching Clint. Mary frowned, tuning in on a closer awareness of Ann.

Clint gave the instrument to Bart as he took off his tie and suit coat and handed them to Dingus. He rolled up his shirt sleeves before he unbuttoned the front of his shirt.

Bart felt tremors of uncertainty, thinking the fountain was next.

But Clint looked at Ann. Other than the fact that his eyes were blue, their dark coloring matched. He took the violin from Bart, put it under his chin, and touched the bow to the strings. The first liquid notes sounded in slow, compelling waves.

Ann raised her hands high above her head, her wrists together, her body postured perfectly. People paused to watch, causing more to stop and stretch to see. A strange hush fell in that small part of the Circle, and the violin's deep, sweet voice was heard more clearly.

The music had a stylized rhythm that held a primitive yearning that was haunting. Clint established it, then nodded to Ann, who began slowly. It was obvious she'd had some training. She was captured by the music and directed by it. Her turns and bendings were graceful, lovely and very stirring. The music and her movements to it called forth pagan longings. She knew she danced for him.

As her body became accustomed to the plaint of unrequited love, she moved more freely, and people backed away to give her more room. She knew Clint's brooding blue gaze followed her, but her black eyes now avoided him. He played with great skill and emotion, and she responded from her very soul. It was beautiful. Their magic created an oasis in that traffic-congested, noisy Friday night in June, in downtown Indianapolis. And it held until the last note.

Her dance completed, Ann returned to her original stance. She blinked to find herself where she was, and her glance fell on Clint, still drawing out the last note to its final whisper.

Suddenly there were noisy comments, friendly cheers and some clapping. Dingus passed the borrowed hat and the man whose hat it was, accompanied the gathering of coins. A cop came along and asked what was going on. Dingus gave him the money for the Patrolmens' Fund, with a dollar's rent to the owner of the hat.

Clint put his jacket back on and smiled at the cheerful urgings for another piece. But screened by the watchers, Ann whispered to Mary, "I must get away." Without questioning, Mary lifted a hand in farewell to Dingus, ignored Clint's shout, and they slipped away through the crowd.

# Two

Mary drove from the firm's reserved parking garage and turned north on Meridian. With an unconscious admission to fleeing, she asked Ann, "What was wrong?"

"I'm not sure. I suppose..." Ann laughed faintly. "I suppose it's my gypsy blood warning me of danger."

Mary didn't laugh. "Clint Burrows is a Getty of the legal world."

"He would be."

"And he's definitely interested in you. Why did I ever take you along?" she teased. "If only I had resisted your clamoring and begging to go."

Ann was silent.

"It's serious? You really have bad vibes?"

"I have a strong feeling of chaos."

"Well." But Mary couldn't think what else to say. She knew better than to scoff.

They drove east for several blocks and then north. Ann's small, white frame house was on a wide lot, and set behind a hedge that was rather close to the street. The lawn was neatly trimmed and there was a high, scalloped board fence, which concealed the large backyard.

Pulling up into the curve of the cracked cement drive, Mary stopped the car and turned to her sister. "Sleep on it. Don't do anything permanently opposed to Clint. It could have been that Sharon's hors d'oeuvres joggled your receptive processes. A little garlic is a dangerous thing."

"I looked down a corridor."

"Well . . ." Mary was stopped for a while. "Whatever it is, this meeting between you two is important. Look down the corridor again."

"Dingus would be good for you."

"He's a good lawyer, but he's not my type. Not enough ambition. A little stiff and formal. But someone should teach him to bend before it's too late. I couldn't believe he went along with us tonight. I couldn't believe *you* did."

"I had no choice."

"Now, don't get spooky on me."

"I can stop this acquaintance with Clint. I don't have to do it. I can pass it by."

"Are you sure you'd want to? How can you know you're right?"

She shook her head in a ridding way.

"Harry was enough emotional turmoil to last me all my life."

"You've never really told me. You just . . . left him. And so strangely. It must have been ghastly to make you simply . . . leave in that way."

"Thank you for not objecting when I asked to leave tonight. I know you wanted to stay."

"Of all the things in this world, you can count on me."

"Ah, Mary. You are so special."

"I know. You owe being here to me. I can tolerate you, too."

"Come by in a day or so. I'm painting something exciting. I want you to see it."

"There are times when I envy you the sensitivity you must endure." Mary watched her. "I see surfaces, I hear words and sounds, I taste food, I smell scents. I feel ordinary emotions. You go so far beyond, that you unnerve me. But I wonder if I'm not blessed to be as ordinary as I am."

"You're extraordinary."

"I love prejudice."

Ann paused in getting out of the car and said, "I'm working on something profound. Come in a couple of days and view my soul."

"Raising you has been an experience."

"Mother and Dad thank God for you every night."

"They're afraid to thank God for you because then He might notice you're missing."

"There's a typical, ordinary, Mary statement."

"Go along and let me go home to my chaste bed."

"Thanks."

"You're welcome."


He came to her place. Ann was lying in her bed in that small house, and the summer moonlight was strong. She knew he was there before she heard his soft knock, and she didn't move. She heard the second gentle tap. It seemed appropriate that he didn't use the bell. She sensed his soundless movement across her porch to the drive, to silently open the gate. He came around the house.

She lay, her eyes moving with his prowling sounds. It was as though a large and curious beast gave its attention to the house. He didn't call to her. He was simply there. She heard the whisper of the grasses as he passed her windows, and heard as he paused, knowing where she lay. He stood there. And they were aware each of the other. He stood for a long time. Then he went away, soundlessly. But suddenly her body relaxed, and she wept, knowing that while he might now be gone, their involvement had begun.

Toward morning Ann dreamed of the misty corridor and knew she should explore farther; but she saw turmoil and came back. She was afraid. Ann was wakened by the dream's emotions, and she had the lingering feeling that the chaos was to...others. Who? To others whom she didn't know. She frowned into the dawn, wondering how her lone life could ever become so entangled with people she didn't know.

She was a solitary woman who rarely sought out her friends. Mary satisfied her scant need for contact. Her parents were indulgent but confused by their changeling. They looked at her drawings and paintings and were amazed. They smiled and kissed her cheek. And she knew there was no touchstone.

Her parents said she was like a strange aunt of her father's. The word *strange* was always connected with that aunt. Her name had been Annette. She'd gone off with her lover to some obscure country Ann had forgotten. They'd died in an uprising before Ann was born. Ann had a picture of her in foreign clothing. And when Ann was troubled, as she was now, she sought Annette's picture, took it from the ancient storage trunk and set in one of the deep window ledges to look at it, wishing they had met, talked. She was so alone.

Clint came before her sister. He came at ten in the morning. He knocked on the door, and she already knew who would be there. She opened the door and stood quite cool and composed in her paint-splattered, purple sleeveless smock. Her hair was in its stern knot, and she didn't smile.

"You're elusive," he told her, not in chiding but in acknowledgement.

"No."

"May I come in?"

"I'm working."

"I've heard you're a painter. I'd like to see your work."

"Are you buying?"

As she lifted her chin, he saw a flicker of humor in her eyes. "Maybe." He smiled a little.

"Then I'll allow you some time." She opened the door and against all good judgment, permitted him inside her sanctuary. The room was blocked by a very tall and remarkable Chinese screen that was delicately, intricately done. He was captured by it, as were most, and she waited patiently as he studied it. His eyes relinquished the treasure, and he came around its edge into the room. It was not neat. The abused floor was bare and scuffed with an occasional splattering of paint.

The walls were covered with paintings, sketches, watercolors, drawings. All of it was remarkably coherent in spite of the lack of planning. Ann's subconscious sense of balance had placed the pictures to form not only the wild array but the negative pattern.

He stood and surveyed the stunning spectacle of her works. He wasn't overwhelmed, because he was a giant in his own field; therefore he didn't feel competitive or threatened, and he could appreciate her talent. He said softly, "My God."

"Most say that in a different tone." She smiled as she looked up at him as a kindred spirit.

While he had sustained his balance through his viewing of her works, it was the feeling that went through him at her accepting smile was what almost overwhelmed him. He had no idea what exactly was happening to him, but he knew he had to see it through. To what end?

His eyes focused on her walls. There were seascapes and winter scenes. There were imaginative ones of emotion and mood, there were those of valor and derring-do, there were children. There was awesome talent.

The sparse furniture was all but buried under the accoutrements of an artist. Piles of very large, heavy papers were on tables, and bookshelves bulged. There were trays of paints in squeezed tubes and fat new ones, and pots with brushes. And facing the tall north windows were several easels with stretched canvases in various stages of completion. There were portraits that looked as if the people had been approached while they were involved with things that interested them.

Ann pulled a cloth over one she'd been working on, and covered it from his sight.

"Don't you sell any?" He looked at the wealth of paintings in the room.

"I'm getting ready for a show."

"You are talented."

"I am blessed."

"Yes." He turned to her then. "Why did you run?"

"You know."

"You're apprehensive for some reason, but why run from me?"

"I see turmoil for us."

He smiled and touched her cheek with one finger. "Don't be afraid. Nothing is gained without some disturbance."

"In my life there's been too much."

"Now, I will be with you. I'll smooth things for you."

She looked at him with clear, seeing eyes. He said "*I will* not *I would*." She corrected him: "You can't be with me. Not all the time."

"But if you need me, I will come to you."

How could he know that? How could he accept all that he implied? "How do you know?"

"I don't. I've never had anything remotely like this happen with me. I stood outside your window last night, knowing exactly where you lay and that you were awake and aware of me. How could that be?" His voice was deep, his blue eyes intense; he wasn't confused, only curious. He had accepted their involvement. "Don't shut me out."

"I'm afraid."

"Of me?"

"Of...the portent. Of what will happen. It might tear me apart."

"No harm will come to you."

"How can you be so sure?" Anguish shadowed her face.

"I wouldn't allow anything to harm you."

"It might be beyond you."

"No." There was no doubt in him.

"This is all very strange."

"I'm a new believer in fate. I saw you, and you winked at me. A lovely, sleek, sophisticated—"

"I have a new contact lens that's remarkable. I've always been very nearsighted in that eye and it's amazing to see so clearly. I close my right eye to see through the lens. I would never wink."

"Fate is triggered by a contact testing?" He laughed with such amusement, his eyes sparkling with his humor. "Well, I suppose if lacking a horseshoe nail could bring down a country, I can be felled by a woman trying out a new contact."

"You are magnificent. I'd like to paint you."

In easy amusement, with no touch of lasciviousness, he inquired, "Nude, in bed, replete?"

"Is that what this is? Sexual desire?"

"It's more than that. You know it, too."

"I'll never marry again."

"Who was the man?"

"Harry Warsaw."

"Him? He isn't dead."

"No."

"Then he's mad to have let you go." He frowned a little. "I've never heard that he was insane. And in his business, that sort of thing gets around." He pierced her with his blue-eyed stare. "Is he?"

She turned away and didn't reply.

"So." The word was a thoughtful conviction. He had accepted that she was innocent. Whatever had happened, it hadn't been because of her. He had given her his trust. "Will I ever know? I need to, if I'm to change your mind about men."

"I'm not wary of men—only of losing my freedom."

"Curiouser and curiouser."

"No. Only caution. Only resolve. I must be free."

"I have a very light hand," he promised her, his eyes serious.

"But a hand, nevertheless."

"A hand can help . . . protect . . . defend."

She turned toward him with a slight smile. But her eyes were guarded.

"I'm not sure how to conduct myself." He grinned at her. "This is an unusual courtship. We're months down the way from our beginning just yesterday, with a testing of your contact. You have to know I had already noticed you. Your ersatz wink only gave me the heart to approach you. You weren't there to meet people and make friends."

"I went for the food."

"In all my life, I've never seen anything so erotic as you tasting those hors d'oeuvres. I wanted you to taste me that way."

"I think you're dangerous."

"No."

"You told me that you are harmless."

"I am."

"You are the center of a maelstrom."

"That's true at the office, but that's business. This is separate."

"You're very quick to calm me, but are you really separate? Or do you simply want to get me into bed?"

"Well . . . I *had* thought of that. Yes, I actually had."

"When you were outside my window?"

He sobered. "Not then, oddly enough. Then it was a very intense…almost communication. Did you feel it?"

"Yes."

He came close to her and put his big hand to the side of her head. Then he watched her involuntary intake of breath, and her eyes slitted against the wave of feeling that went through both of them. It was beyond sexual attraction. His face was still as he withstood the amazing sweep of whatever it was that rocked them. Softly he asked, "What is this? What in the world is happening? You feel it, too."

She only nodded.

"What do you want me to do?" His question gave her control, not only of him but of their future.

She smiled ruefully. "It's too late."

"I knew that last night."

"I thought I could escape any entanglement with you."

"No. Nor can I. I need to kiss you." His voice was husky.

"I don't think I can cope with a kiss."

"I'll try a very small one first."

Her eyes opened wide with her acknowledgment of his last word. It would be their first of many, but this one would be small.

He leaned his face down to hers, watching intently, his breathing uneven, his muscles tensing. And his mouth touched her lips, gently. It was devastating. He drew in a ragged breath, wrapping his arms around her, pulling her tightly to him. The kiss was out of his control; it was consuming her.

She wept, clinging, straining to him. And she said, "It's been so long." Why had she said that?

He hesitated just a second. "What?"

She gulped. "I don't know." Their eyes met. He'd thought—what? He smiled, and his kiss was tender.

They parted at last, their hands trailing off the other as they moved back in minute, reluctant separations. He asked, "Do you do anything so mundane as to eat ordinary food? I'm human. I need food."

"Right away?"

"As soon as possible."

"Come into the kitchen. I'll feed you." She led him through the cluttered studio into a pristine kitchen— orderly, clean. She ground the coffee beans for brewing before she made him an omelet. She gave him rolls that were light, flaky, perfect, and slyly filled with apricots and pecans.

They melted in his mouth and he licked the crumbs from his lips. She laughed. He asked, "The caterer?"

She shook her head. "No. I made them."

"You are an artist."

"I love food."

By then the the kitchen was cluttered with bowls and pans and utensils. He said, "I'll help clean up."

"No. Mable comes and helps. I pay her well. I dislike making it tidy again."

"I'm an experienced busboy. I'd do my share."

"I'll remember that."

"May I see your room—where you were last night?"

"Not now."

"I can wait for you. Just let me see the room."

"It, too, is untidy."

"I want to see where you dream."

She understood that was different from just seeing her bed. She was reluctant, but she took him through the little hall to the one bedroom in the small house. "Imagine building a one-bedroom house."

"It's a large one. Beautiful. The pictures are magnificent. I'd like that one." It was of a castle. A cone hat on the battlements indicated a woman who was surrounded and beleaguered. Only the rescuing hero's arm was seen on the left, as if the viewer looked from low behind him, as if he stood while his followers were concealed. The arm's mailed fist was clenched. Clint turned to Ann. "You?"

"How did you know?"

He indicated the fist. "That is I."

"You would rescue me?"

He seemed impatient with the redundant question. "Yes."

"From what?"

"From..." He regarded her from narrowed eyes. "From yourself."

"How did you know?"

"I don't know. I only guessed. You painted that after the divorce."

"Yes."

"It was the divorce that trapped you in a besieged castle?"

"The marriage."

"Why didn't the divorce free you?"

"I don't know."

"I will, you know. You must be free for me." He was very positive. He turned and looked around the room. At the unmade feminine bed with its chiffon drapery in pink. At the pure white sheets and the light coverlet of silk. At the heavily lace-edged pillows. It was barely disturbed. How strange that after their encounter last night, she'd slept so still. His bed had been torn apart by his restlessness.

"Where is your home?" she asked.

"Right now I've a condo in the renovated Lockerbee Glove Factory. Most recently, I'm from Chicago. I have family there. A brother and sister-in-law. Their two kids."

"We have some family around. We aren't very prolific."

"Tell me about this painting." It was an abstract.

"If I must explain it, then I've failed to communicate."

After her words, he looked more closely and saw the restless colors. He asked, "Are you that unsettled?"

"Not now. I've made a small, private place for myself that's peaceful. In it, I'm safe and free. That's why I resist your intrusion."

"You believe I'm intruding? I thought I was the rescuer."

"I've walled up my castle."

"A walled castle is isolated."

"From disruption," she agreed. "From suffering, from disappointment."

"From living," he corrected.

"I've tried living and it's dreadful."

He watched her, pushing his lower lip out thoughtfully. "You're not a quitter."

"Yes. I can't bear the emotion of contention."

"Must there be contention?"

"It's there."

"Not with us," he said emphatically.

"Even then."

"We can't turn back."

She sighed. "I know."

"It'll be all right. Trust me."

"I have no trust left."

"You let me in your house. That proves something. We'll work on that until you feel safe and can open your gates." He waited, but she didn't say anything. He looked again at her bedside clock. "I should leave. I've an appointment. Would you like me to stay?"

Again he put power over him in her hands. She did consider asking him to stay, but it would only be so that she could use that power. If she did, he would, now. "Not this time."

"Kiss me goodbye."

"Next time."

He knew she wasn't tormenting him. She really didn't think she could handle another kiss. He disciplined himself not to touch her.

She led him through the hodgepodge of supplies, paintings and boxes to the door. She opened it for him and stood aside.

He had a hard time forcing himself to leave her. In spite of her disturbance, she was reluctant that he go. But it was better that he leave.

"I'll be by later."

She looked up at him and understood. She nodded, and he left. She closed the door and leaned her head against it almost in despair. It had begun. Whatever was fated would happen. She had no choice. Would she survive? What about Clint? She had to protect him, too.

As Clint left, Ann's great monster of a yellow cat, entered through the briefly opened door. He made his way through the jumbled rooms, sniffing the smell of the alien male intruder and acting disgruntled. Ann took him into the kitchen and gave him a chicken liver, which he consented to nibble.

Mac had found a field mouse, so he could make his "slave" anxious about his appetite. Having eaten enough so that she wouldn't panic about him and take him to the vet, he took his battle-scarred body to her bed and cleaned himself, indifferent to the hair balls left on the pink silken coverlet.

Ann went back to the studio and threw back the cloth that covered her painting. This one was her soul. She pulled her stool to the window and sat studying the painting for a long time. It was in sepia shadows and at first appeared only as a stylized abstract. She went to it and began reworking the lower left corner. Her soul was changing?

When Mary came that afternoon with orders that Ann come to their parents' house for dinner on the following Sunday, Ann showed her sister the painting.

Mary wasn't subtle. "I know it's pithy as all bloody hell, but I do get a sense of vast plots that scare me a little. The diminishing arm here in the bottom corner makes me wonder what's coming off."

"It isn't diminishing. It's gathering strength."

"Oh." Mary frowned at it for a while, then looked up at Ann. "Is this the arm in the other picture? *The Hero?*"

"Maybe."

"Clint?"

"Perhaps."

"Is this what scares you?"

"Yes."

"We could go to England for a while. I have some time coming."

"It would only delay it all."

"That bad?"

"I don't know."

"Are you going to see Clint again?"

"I have no choice."

"Oh, yes you do, too, have a choice!" Mary was vigorously militant. "You're a free woman! You don't have to do anything that you don't want to do!" She stood riveted for a while, very earnest. But then humor crept into her eyes as she went on, "Except, of course, you do have to go home on Sunday for dinner. I think Mother has a candidate for us. I thought I'd warn you of that in case you know anyone whose kids could give you a quick case of measles or chicken pox?"

"You handle this one. I rebuffed the last one."

"I'm taking Dingus. It gave Mother the quivers when I asked to invite him. They'll love him. That ought to kill off this madness right away."

"Do you want it killed off?"

"He intrigues me," Mary admitted. "I believe it's because he's so stiff. I could unbend him and widen his life. He's much too involved in law. He needs to know there are other things in life. But he is a good man. He works hard."

Ann was silent.

Mary hastened to assure her, "I'm not getting serious or dewy-eyed or anything like that."

Ann gave her a thoughtful study, which Mary ignored with a good deal of self-consciousness.

It was late in the afternoon when Clint called. "Let's have supper out."

"I bought shrimp and tenderloins."

"Let's eat at your place!"

"I gave Mac one of the shrimps and he thinks they're okay."

There was a slight pause. "Who is Mac?"

"The cat who owns me."

"Only for a time."

"That's what I'm afraid of." She wasn't teasing. He would possess her.

He dismissed her fears. "There's no reason for you to be afraid. I'll be there. I'll bring wine. Any druthers?"

"Choose."

"With a choice, I'd choose you."

"I could be poison."

"I'd die happy."


She wore a long silk gown that skimmed her body. It was dark blue with large red polka dots and red stripes at the plunging neckline, around the sleeveless edges, and in a border at the hem. Her gypsy-black hair was in a single braid down her back, and she was barefoot.

Waiting for Clint, Ann was filled with tension, which made her restless. She paced, wiping her palms down her hips, while Mac watched. When Clint arrived, she was seemingly cool and calm. Clint and Mac exchanged a measuring glance, and each dismissed the other.

Clint set the wine on the kitchen table and presented Ann with a bouquet of gladiolus. She found a great pot and took the flowers out to the table at the side of the house. It was his first daylight glimpse of the backyard, and it did surprise him.

She had let it go wild. There were all sorts of weeds mixed with English-garden-style plantings. There was a child-protecting grid covering a twelve-by-eight foot pond, which contained goldfish. On the cement border around the pond stood a metal table and chairs. There were brick paths through the flower/weed combinations, and the trees spread their limbs over and around so that the yard was shaded and quite lovely.

"Your gardener quit?"

"I have the front yard mowed as a concession to the neighbors. This is mine. Before I bought this house, it had stood empty almost fifteen years. I bought it for all the young trees that had volunteered to grow back here. Look at the variety!"

With some surprise he commented, "It's quite charming."

"I once read in a romance that weeds were simply unloved flowers. Have you ever looked closely at a dandelion? They are exquisite."

There was a wide board swing hanging from a tall maple and there was a porch swing hung from a tall pipe wired to sturdy limbs. A hammock was between two trees near the surrounding tall wooden fence. He grinned at her. "I suppose the fact that Mac is really a jungle cat had nothing to do with your keeping this place for him?

"It's for me. This is me. It's free. Unmanicured. Untamed."

"I don't want to tame you," he assured her softly.

"I wouldn't fit into your world."

"Then I'd change the world."

"You might." She arranged his gladiolus on the table by the pond. She removed the pot of begonias and set them on the edge of the tiled lip of the pond.

They both looked at his flowers: they were incongruously formal there in that carelessly beautiful setting.

# Three

In the days that followed, Ann and Clint figuratively circled each other, as would alien creatures. She was drawn to him, but wary, while he tried to coax her from behind her defenses.

She was as elusive as smoke; as haunting. Yet, like smoke on a still day, she lingered. It wasn't her presence that she denied Clint, it was her essence. She seemed forever out of reach, although she was there.

As with any power man, Clint's free time was severely limited. He traveled to other cities for consultations. There was his caseload, and while his associates worked on the nitty-gritty, he still had to be informed, to coordinate their efforts; and he had to be in court.

He came to Ann at odd times of the day and night. Never again did she conceal herself from him in silence, as she had that first night. She was there for him. But she was not completely open or accepting. She was still beyond his grasp.

He made her laugh. He lay in her hammock and suggested she wave peacock plumes over his tree-shaded body during the lazy summer days. And she actually dropped grapes into his opened mouth, making his eyes sparkle and his hands itch to hold her.

Clint took great pleasure in washing and vacuuming Ann's car; but careless as she was, she didn't know to be impressed with his labors.

He had never been anyplace where he'd felt so serene—or so frustrated. He dreamed of making love to her in that untamed yard. He could have coaxed her into submission, and she would have yielded, but he wanted more than her body. He watched her and wondered how long it would take.

He brought his own violin and played for her on rainy days as she painted, or he played his music in the sun-dappled Eden she'd contrived in the backyard.

The first time Clint played his violin, Mac the cat came to listen. He was very alert, sitting up and listening. He moved his head, watching the bow on the strings, and was fascinated.

With the cat showing such great attention to the music, Ann decided it was the catgut used in the strings that struck a chord. The cat's interest was probably genetic in felines.

Clint listened to Ann's explanation and blinked a couple of times before he said "Oh." And he made Ann laugh.

Gradually, as the days passed, she touched Clint more. Her gaze rested on him, and she began to do sketches of him. He allowed her any freedom, but he carefully disciplined himself. His hands. His words. His manner.

He dreamed of her, waking and sleeping. His concentration was broken and undisciplined. He watched her hands move and wanted them on him. He watched her eat, and wanted her mouth on him. He watched her body and wanted his hands on her. She drove his body frantic, and his mind seemed able to think of nothing else but her.

It was exquisite torture to be with her, to hear her voice as it moved from his ear into his soul. Her voice was perfect. Her smile healed all the wounds his ego had ever endured, and when she touched him, it was like a magic caress.

It was only stern control that kept his hands reasonably impersonal. He never slid one from her throat to her breast. He ruled himself harshly. He never smoothed a hand over her sassy bottom; tempted as he was, he never did it.

But he looked at her. He squirmed inside his body as his hungry study of her went lurid and erotic. But he didn't touch her.

Well, he did smooth her hair. He put a hand on her shoulder. He held her hand. He plucked a seeming straw from her hair and discarded it before she even saw that it was nothing. And he took her arm and "helped" her to mount the three steps to the French doors.

But he never touched her as he longed to do. He dreamed of touching her, of making love to her. He slept poorly. He didn't mind. The distraction was all he had of her.

One peaceful day, as they lay in the grasses and watched the butterflies, she told him, "You are a beast under stern restraint."

His surprise at her words caused a burst of laughter that was rueful, and he shook his head, as if helpless.

She rose up on one elbow in order to see his face. "Why does my knowing that make you laugh?"

"I thought I was being so brilliantly subtle, so perfectly controlled, while I'm about to explode because I want you so badly. I was so smug, I thought I had you fooled. How did you know?"

"Your breathing. You're so tightly coiled. You pretend to relax, but your body is tense. Your small movements are too quick. Your long movements are studied, they aren't impulsive."

"That blows my career on the stage."

"I would let you have me."

"Oh, Ann—"

"I know this hasn't been easy for you. I would help you to survive. I don't want you to hang on in hope of surcease. I'll give it to you." With the decision, she stood, pulled her long cotton dress off over her head, and spread it on the ground. She lay down on it, on her back, and held still in the dappling sunlight.

Quick realizations came to Clint. She'd never been courted into loving, nor had she ever instigated love...and obviously, she had never enjoyed a coupling. He was appalled.

With her stripping off her gown, desire had flooded his already half-aroused body. That had been his constant state since he'd first seen her. Now his hands trembled, his breathing became ragged, and he began to sweat. He knew he couldn't make love with her—

not now; not if he wanted their lives to progress as they should.

She didn't want love from him; she wanted to give him "surcease," peace. She wasn't even going to make love to him. It was only an act to give him physical release. Yet she was willing to allow him that. She was giving him her body. And he could not take her. Not like this.

But he would have to be very tactful in declining her gift. How could he survive the necessary tenderness he must give her in refusing her? How could he control himself? He could go over to the pond and sit in the cooling water with the goldfish. He could climb the trees; or better yet, he could try to uproot a couple of them. He could tear his hair out and yell bloody murder. He could...

She opened her eyes, and without moving her head, she strained to see him. She saw that he concentrated on her, and he appeared to be very disturbed. She closed her eyes tightly and went rigid.

She was afraid? What sort of man was Harry Warsaw? In studying Ann, Clint understood that she wasn't terrified, just braced to endure. Think of that. She was willing to allow him to take her body in the most intimate way; and all that it would be, to her, was an endurance. How absolutely terrible for any woman to endure such an exquisite act with...endurance.

It was his compassion that rescued him. It didn't help to ease his desire, but it made him think first of her. He reached out a hand and laid it on her arm. She flinched. And he said, "Oh, my love, what did he do to you?"

"Nothing." She opened her eyes. "He was very quick about it."

"My God."

"No, no. It hurt very little. It was soon over. You can go ahead. I know what it's like. I can stand it. I don't mind. Just don't make me wait so long. I get too tense, and then it hurts more."

"It shouldn't hurt at all." He was so angry at her clumsy ex-husband that his words were harsh. "It should feel very nice. You should be able to enjoy it, to want to make love."

"That's what he said. He said I was frigid. Don't get mad at me. I won't fight you."

All her words tore at him. He put his head in his hands to try to control the need to smash an absent man. How could any man have used Ann so badly? Ann. She was his first concern. His own feelings must be pushed aside.

Moving slowly in order to be unthreatening, he eased to his side, closer to her, and he said, "You're beautiful. Let me look at you."

Still lying stiffly with her eyes closed, she said quickly, "All right. But don't take too long. I'm really very nervous."

"There isn't time today for me to make love with you and—"

"Yes. It'll only take a couple of minutes. Go ahead and get it over with."

Clint wondered if she closed her eyes to remove herself from the act? He smoothed his hand along her arm. "No, it will take a while for me to love you, because I want our first time to be perfect. I want you to enjoy it, too."

She was agitated. She took several breaths to speak but didn't, and finally, shaking her head, she said, "I really don't like doing it. I'm not sure he really did. It

was more a compulsion for him. But I just couldn't....
I just ... It isn't something I like.''

"Then I won't do it. Not until you ask me to make
love to you."

Her troubled gaze came to him. Her voice was hesitant and regretful, but the words were positive. "Then
we never will."

"I'm not sure you understand how very much I am
coming to love you. I couldn't leave you even if we
never make love."

"But...wouldn't it be...very difficult for you? Why
would you still stay? Isn't that the only reason men
need women? For release?"

"I suppose not knowing about making love is like
missing phonetics. To understand the words, you have
to start all over with sounds. You are abysmally un-
schooled in love, my love. You have to start all over.
We'll begin with the basics. You're a woman. You're
lovely, eye-filling and desirable. I'm a man. I'm
equipped to give you pleasure and children. Men call
women chattels, but it's an ego thing. It's really the
other way around. We're slaves of women. I hate to
take a perfectly good woman and allow her to realize
her power, but you're missing too much of life. And
without you, I'll miss it, too."

Very seriously, she replied, "I told you I didn't
mind. You can go ahead. I do understand."

"When..." He had trouble actually saying Harry's name. "When he kissed you, did you feel the way
you do with my kisses?"

"He wasn't affectionate. If he weren't going to have
sex, he didn't like to be touched. Or kissed or hugged.
He would squirm away. Or push me away. When we
were first married, I tried. I had seen people kiss and

I would have liked to be hugged that way, but he didn't like it."

"You let me hug you."

"Yes. I like it—with you."

"Let me just hug you for a while. I promise I won't take you. Relax. Let's just be easy together."

"I'll put my dress back on. Sorry."

"Sorry?"

"He never liked to see me naked. I embarrassed him unless—"

"I would like you to go around without clothes all the time. You are exquisite."

"Really?"

"Oh, Ann, look at you!" He was by then so concerned for her that he had the strength to survive this ordeal. Too much rode on his care of her now. He moved a gentle hand over her stomach as he said, "How lovely your skin feels to my hand. You're so beautiful. This pretty line from your navel and this fluff. Ahh." But her skin had goose bumps and her muscles were rigid. "I won't hurt you."

"My... breasts are tender."

"Time for your period?" He smiled gently, sharing that intimacy.

She went scarlet. "No. But he squeezed too hard." She looked up sharply and brought her hands up so quickly that he realized she had been forcing herself not to defend her body.

"He... abused you?"

"No, no. He was just... rough. When I cried, he would be furious. He said if I wasn't so frigid, I would like it."

In concise words, Clint mentally consigned Harry to some spectacular punishments.

Ann went on: "I asked my doctor about it. I thought maybe he was being unreasonable, but she agreed with him. She said that with foreplay, a woman can be passionate enough to be handled differently. Not roughly, but less gently. She explained so that I would know the difference. It was no more than Harry did. I'm frigid." She gave him a mournful look.

"You don't kiss 'frigid.'"

"I've never kissed anyone the way I kiss you. You...enjoy it so, and you help. You make me feel as if I'm a part of the kiss."

"That's the way love is, and that's how coupling should be. I want very badly to love you. But I won't until you ask me. Just let me hold you and kiss you."

"I don't mind, if you . . . go ahead."

"I want you hungry for me."

"Clint, that may never be. What then?"

"We'll handle that problem if that time comes."

She burst into noisy tears! He was appalled. "What is it? Shh, shh. Nothing's that bad. Ah, honey. Oh, my love. Shh. You're all right. I'm here, and nothing bad can happen to you. Shh." Slowly, slowly, he gathered her to him and soothed her. He sat up, drew her across his body and rocked her in his arms. But her tears went on. He finally picked her up and carried her to the porch swing under the trees and sat with her on his lap as he swung them slowly, comforting her.

In hiccups and shaky breaths she said, "I was so afraid."

"Of me? How could you be afraid of your hero? I'm your protector. You can't ever be afraid of me."

"I've shunned contact with men. I wasn't ever going to come out of my secret place. You've been intruding, and I was afraid it would all begin again. Yet with you I couldn't draw away. This has been a terrible time for me."

"Why didn't you tell me?"

"I didn't know I could."

He groaned as he hugged her close to him. "Ann, for God's sake, don't shut me out. How can I solve your problems if I don't know what they are?"

Her breathing still jerky from her tears, she lay naked in his arms. He held her, keeping the swing in slow, soothing motion. In the silence, his concern for her weakened as his consciousness of her nudity was brought strongly to his body's attention. He willed his hands not to move, but his hot mouth sought hers.

He kissed her, using all his skill. He coaxed and teased. His scalding tongue slipped along her tightly closed lips. He flicked it there and coaxed for entrance, but he didn't insist. He turned his tongue's talents to her ear, and she gasped and shivered. She was still tense. He rubbed his face into the side of her neck and kissed her shoulder. He held her close against him, wishing his shirt would vanish.

Had he known what would follow, he would have removed his shirt when she first took off her dress. For him to get rid of it now would be too threatening to her. But she was so soft against him. Women were built so miraculously holdable. She felt so good to him. It was exquisite pain. But he was very conscious of the fact that she had never relaxed. She was still braced.

He thought ruefully that he should have a medal for valor. He loosened his arms, squinting his eyes and clenching his teeth, and he admitted, "I'm a shambles."

She raised bleak eyes to his and said again, "You could go ahead."

Win the battle, but lose the war. That was what would happen. If he ever could have her love, freely given, he would have to endure now. He grinned at her, his teeth still clenched, and told her, "Get off all my legs and let me up. I need to lift a tree or two."

"Why would you do that?" She unfolded her long, slender legs and rose to stand modestly, half turned away.

"It won't solve anything, but it does help." He stood and walked stiffly to the house and gave a good try at moving the side of it up and over.

She had picked up her gown and was shaking it out. "You are very different," she said with some confusion.

He turned quickly to her. "There! Remember that! It's important for you to understand that very thing. I am a different man."

"I know that!" She pulled the dress over her head and settled it. "I *told* you that you could go ahead!"

"I don't *want* to 'go ahead' and 'do it.' That's the point I'm trying to make with you. I want to *share* love with you."

"Then go ahead and get it over with! You don't make sense!"

"I'm going to teach you the difference between 'getting it over' and making love."

"I'm unteachable. Harry tried for almost two years. I couldn't learn."

His voice harsh, Clint told her, "Harry was no teacher. He was a user."

Ann's eyes widened as she looked startled. She wasn't stupid. She understood what Clint had said; it was just that it was an oblique slant on ingrained thinking.

It wasn't her fault; it was Harry's? She'd never once considered that. She had accepted all the blame for the entire disaster. Could Harry have some of the blame? Perhaps. But it still came down to the basic fact that she was frigid. Had she been able to endure Harry with more grace, there might have been no other problems.

Her head went down and her fragile figure was defeated. He asked, "What are you thinking?"

She was frigid and untidy. To be a failure in the basics of marriage was humiliating for a woman. "That I've failed you."

"You mean if I'd hopped aboard that stiff, submitting woman, I would have won? Won what?"

It was as if he'd slapped her. How often had Harry said almost the same words? Her bleak eyes came to Clint's and she said, "At least you would have had relief."

"And you?" he demanded. "What would you have had? What, besides a sore body?"

Whether she received anything from the act had never come into any discussion. He surprised her. "I'm incapable. I get nothing from it. I give."

"Bless Harry's shriveled-up, little bitty soul. He let you participate in an 'act.' Sounds exciting. Didn't he ever make love to you?"

"I said you could. Why are you so mad at me? You're just like Harry."

He took long strides to her and grasped her upper arms with his hands. "No! Never." He wrapped his arms around her and hugged her furiously. "I'm not mad at you. I'm . . . I'm . . ." He sought an acceptable word. "I'm ticked off that you've been so badly used. I can't believe this could happen to any woman in this day and age. How long have you been divorced?"

"Almost three years. I was married at twenty. I'm almost twenty-six."

"Don't you ever read anything? Haven't you heard about women and foreplay and orgasms and love? It's your body. Haven't you ever been curious how it works?"

"It didn't work that way for me."

"This doctor you went to, did she examine you?"

"Of course."

"Did you go to any counselor? Therapist?"

"They said it was up to me. Harry wouldn't go."

"Let me guess. He said it was *your* problem."

"Yes."

"Well, I'm going to get some advice. Want to come along?"

"I've been 'adviced' out. I don't have problems anymore. I'm safe from them. Without you, I could be contented as I am. I release you. This won't ever work."

"I'm not so fainthearted. I'll be back. I find you excruciatingly desirable." He grinned at her.

She gave him a sober look. "You're not the only man who has looked at me in that way."

"Then you've been with other men besides Harry?"

"No. With the problem I have, I've never been tempted."

"I like a challenge." He smiled.

"Let me go. Let me be the way I was before I met you."

"I can't."

"You'll only exhaust us both and make us miserable."

"We'll be friends. Kissing friends, but only that. I won't ask any more of you."

"That isn't a normal relationship for you. You need a woman."

"I'll manage."

"Oh, Clint, I wish . . ." She didn't know what she wished, only knew that she was terribly distressed for him.

"At least you aren't indifferent."

"I wish I knew what to do."

"Enjoy me as a friend. Think of things to tell me. Listen to me. Let me hold you and kiss you."

"I can do that." She watched him uncertainly.

"So can I, my princess in the tower, so can I. Let me hold you close while I tell you goodbye."

"Oh, Clint." Her words were said almost in despair. But she met him halfway, and she hugged him back, lying against him, soft and pliant.

His kisses were chaste, but they lingered. She lifted her mouth and kissed him back. He held her unthreateningly, until his body was on the verge of revolt. Then he released himself. Did she realize how she clung to him?

Ann's gallery show loomed. She worked with feverish restlessness, but when Clint came, she smiled and took the time for him. He wondered if she was aware she did that. He was more important to her than her work. He was careful not to be selfish with her time. But it gave him great hope that she didn't hurry him away.

So he tried not to interfere with her schedule. He tried to fit in so that he could be there while she continued to work. That way, he could be with her, watch her, and not feel he was taking advantage of her courtesy.

One way was his music. He played his violin for her as she painted, and that pleased her. She would request the mood she wanted, not the particular piece, for music was an obscure field to her. It gave him pleasure to give her the music.

And Clint went downtown with Ann, to examine Jon Hays's gallery on Massachusetts Avenue, where her show was to be held. It was a street of small shops, and there were other galleries along the way.

Clint was critical of the gallery. He said, "The space is too small."

"Too small? How many paintings do you think I have?"

"A studio chock-full," he replied. "This place will never hold all your pictures."

"Phooey," Ann said. "It's quite big enough. It suits me."

"How about renting the Hoosier Dome?"

She rolled her eyes and sighed.

He hired a van for transferring her paintings to the gallery. And there were two burly men to help her move her pictures from her studio. Then he contrived a free day to help her hang her pictures for the show. No greater friend was there, in all the universe, than a patient one who lent muscle and strength to an artist who was plotting and changing the hanging of a show. Clint was fascinated. He watched, amazed that where the pictures were hung changed the perception of the viewer.

And Clint saw to it that she drank enough water and that she remembered to eat. He solved that by seeing to it that food arrived where she was at the time.

"You're marvelous," she told him while eating a Coney dog that evening.

Clint could see that she wasn't paying any real attention to the chill frankfurter in the soft bun. But he watched as she flicked her tongue to catch an elusive bit of onion, and the sight of that tongue made a tingle go along him. He observed, "Chablis and hot dogs. Exactly what any exhausted woman needs." He was inordinately pleased that he'd pleased her.

"The show will be brilliant," she told Clint with flair.

"It already is, was, will be."

She nodded smugly. "It's perfectly hung. You were magnificently patient. You never complained. Even Jon left."

"You did it exactly right."

"Yes." She smiled in satisfaction.

He watched her. Someday it would be he who made her that contentedly tired.

She asked him, "How did you ever manage to get today free?"

"Ruthlessly," he admitted.

"I appreciate you."

"Geniuses must always be helped with the mundane things in their lives, along with the important things. Today was important. I may not always be able to make it, but either I will be there, or someone equally attentive—but not too." He grinned as he added that.

*And she leaned and kissed him!*

It was the first time that she'd ever made any gesture voluntarily. He was so moved that he felt his eyes prickle with starting tears. He grinned at her and said, "You can't get away with only that sweet payment. I need another."

Quite as if she always did it, she lifted her arms and hugged him. She cradled her head against his throat, by his shoulder, and she held him so wonderfully that he was thrilled almost motionless. His arms had automatically enclosed her, and he stood there, riveted with desire. She leaned her head back to smile into his serious face, then she moved up his body as she stood on her toes, and she kissed him again softly, sweetly.

When she released him and slid back that inch or so along his very sensitive body, he cleared his throat and asked, "How soon before you have another show?"

She patted his hair back and said, "Not until next year."

"Oh." That stymied him briefly. "Well, I must say that it will take at least a day to get all those pictures *unhung.* So I'll be here when the show's finished in a month."

"Maybe I won't have to take them down. If they sell, then the buyers will remove them."

Gloomily he responded, "There's no question that they'll all sell."

Puzzled she asked, "Why does that disappoint you?"

"If they sell, I can't help you take them down, and I won't get a gratitude kiss."

She laughed in genuine amusement. "I'll kiss you for each one sold."

"Done! You already owe me two. I'll show you the two I want."

She was very curious about which he'd choose and went with him to see. One was very small, a filler she'd hung for balance. It was of a fisherman on the White River. The seemingly untamed riverway held an earnest, concentrated male who was fishing. The figure was little more than a streak of color in the natural scene. It was peaceful, restful, too small really to be considered anything but a thank-you gift to someone special.

The second one Clint chose was another matter. It was intricately done; therefore it took some study. And each time it was studied, more would be found. It was cunningly plotted, in a monotone like her soul-painting in sepia. This was of the sea and done in a sea green.

He wrote the check for it, and she gave him a "sold" sticker to put on the frame. She gave him the small painting as a gift. He accepted it. Since she kissed him for the sold painting, he kissed her for the gift. And his eyes were blue glints. Did she know she'd reached for him?

# Four

———

At Ann's house a couple of mornings before the opening, Ann told Mary, "I made a deal with Sharon. I did a watercolor of her son, Greg, and in return, she's going to cater the opening."

"If people know Sharon is catering your opening," Mary said thoughtfully, "they'll think you've hit it big."

"Not necessarily. They could just assume I share the best. Food, and incidentally, my paintings."

"You are a very astute woman."

"I was relentlessly raised by my sister Mary."

Mary nodded. "That Mary Moore is another astute woman. Part of success is to latch onto the shooting stars and claim credit."

"Speaking of shooting stars, how is Dingus McGee?" Ann inquired. Then she chuckled a little. "You know, every time I say his whole name, I think of the Robert Service poem, 'The Cremation of Sam Magee.' Did you ever read that?"

"I go for limericks."

"It's close."

"Speaking of shooting stars—" Mary stole Ann's opening "—how is Clint? I was very impressed by how patient he was yesterday, as you changed the hangings."

"Were you there?"

"I *knew* I wouldn't get any credit. You're so absorbed in placing the paintings that you don't see anything else. I brought the Coney dogs and—"

"I remember." Ann was surprised.

"And I went for more wire."

"Oh, yes! We had to wait."

"He must love you."

"I believe it's still only that he is intrigued. He's never been so frustrated or hampered in his life. He can't solve me, and I suffer for him because he won't quit."

"Quit?" Mary frowned.

"It's hopeless between us. Doomed."

"Sounds Victorian."

"For this problem to fit into a time slot, think how dreadful the Victorian age must have been to earn such a labeling."

"What problem?"

"I can't face another relationship. I still foresee chaos if we continue to see each other."

With her more mature, year-and-a-half older wisdom, Mary said, "I think the smooth relationship between a man and a woman must be so rare as to fall through the cracks, and no one ever realizes love can go smoothly."

"So it doesn't go smoothly for you and Dingus?"

"Why would you think there is anything between Dingus and me?"

"You refuse to talk about him."

"As you do with Clint. I wish Dingus would go away."

"He pesters you?"

"No." Mary walked idly in the now almost empty studio. "Actually, he's easily distracted by his work. Something comes up at his office and he becomes so engrossed in solving it that he won't call. He forgets me. Then he arrives on my doorstep and acts as if we should be delighted to see each other."

"And you aren't?"

Mary vowed gloomily, "I would gladly do him bodily harm."

"You're too short and don't weigh enough. You would look ridiculous trying."

"But it would be enormously satisfying, because *then* I would have his attention!"

"You'll probably marry him," Ann commented thoughtfully.

"Don't be adolescent." Mary was irritated and restless.

So, increasingly, was Ann restless. She had no idea what was wrong. She had been so peaceful. Nothing had really changed. She still lived in her quiet niche. Her house and yard were her sanctuary, the cat her stimulating irritation so that she didn't become too placid. She still painted with oblivious concentration. But she was no longer contented.

Why? She searched for the answer and could find no reason. Her life was exactly as it had always been. No. It wasn't. There was one different thing in her life, and it was Clint. Clint? No, this didn't concern Clint. Since Ann felt she was uninvolved with him, she eliminated him as the cause of her dissatisfaction.

Unlike Dingus with Mary, Clint at least called her every day. If he couldn't be there, he called her several times. His deep voice would say, "I wish I was with you." He would say, "I was thinking of you lying in the grasses and flowers and weeds, a wood nymph." He would say, "I was missing you."

So it couldn't be Clint. It must be the show. Yes. Her progressive tension must be about the show. The opening was Friday night, with an invitation wine-and-cheese party. How many would be there? How would they receive her year's labor? Would they be polite? Or would they chat among themselves and ignore the paintings hung on the walls?

Last year's show had been her first, and she'd managed it quite well. Why should she be so hyper this year? She would survive this one. No one was going to stone her. How could she feel so vulnerable? It was ridiculous. She sighed and paced and wrung her hands.

Finally, to exorcise her turmoil, she pulled a bound board from a stack and began to sketch on the surface. She mixed tempera paints on a white enamel butcher's meat tray and painted. Sitting on her high stool, with the board flat on her only slightly tilted drawing table, she painted a picture of an artist at her opening. All the exaggeratedly drawn people were laughing, talking, eating, drinking; and no one looked at any of the paintings. She entitled it *Rave Reviews*.

But, without even hesitating, she set it aside and took heavy watercolor paper from the pile on the bookcase. She cleaned her brushes and put the tempera paints aside. With accelerating eagerness, she took a clean tray and began to squeeze watercolors onto the neutral surface.

She filled the bathtub with several inches of water and dipped the almost-linen paper into the tub and allowed it to drain briefly. Then she laid it on the butcher paper that covered her flattened drawing table, and began a portrait of Clint. She depicted the challenging position of his head, his level blue eyes as they looked when he was watching her. She drew his hair as it was windblown in the garden. And she made his mouth so perfectly chiseled above his stubborn chin.

She judiciously controlled the running colors with a clean cloth. As the paper began to dry, she went in with a tiny brush and India ink. She rinsed the brush in dirty water and blotted it on a cloth, then dipped it into clean water and flicked it dry—pointing the brush hairs perfectly—and the splattering water landed on the abused floor.

At noon Clint found her there. He had his own key by then, and he didn't distract her from her work. He watched her. She raised her eyes, as to a model and changed a line; she looked again, and strengthened another line. She dropped more color into the drying tint and watched as it soaked in with lessening abandon.

She finished and sat back in satisfaction. She raised her arms high, stretched her tired body and smiled at Clint.

She made his body react in the same old way. Why couldn't he be immune to that thrill? What about familiarity breeding indifference? He went to her and kissed her soft lips before he looked at his portrait.

It was how she saw him. Was he so arrogant and hard? No, it was determination. She would know that he was, indeed, determined. And a man of steel. He wasn't that handsome. She saw him as good-looking? Had his hair ever been so artfully tangled? His eyes were that blue. Women talked about his eyes. He said, "You've got me." And his words weren't about the picture.

Then she showed him *Rave Reviews*.

He laughed. "Where's the artist?"

And her finger located the shriveled, depleted figure.

"Is this your nightmare? Do you think this is going to happen to you? Haven't you looked at the beautiful works you've hung? They're all down there waiting to amaze all those who'll see them. How can you feel insecure?"

"It's the nightmare of everyone who must depend on public approval—on strangers, busy people with other lives. We have to snare the attention of those whose lives are lived so fast they haven't the time to see. Or listen. Or taste. Even Sharon must worry if anyone actually tastes her remarkable marvels."

Clint shook his head. "You'll taste. Sharon should watch only you."

"If today is any indication, tomorrow my stomach won't accept anything. I've never been this apprehensive. It's ridiculous."

"You've already sold one painting," he reminded her. "To me."

"Ah, but you're still trying to influence me in your favor. The money wasn't a problem for you. You did it for the kiss."

He was unruffled. "Yes. There's probably nothing you could set me to do, that I wouldn't do if you kissed me. And if you loved me, I could tackle the impossible."

Quietly she reminded him, "You know that you can have me, anytime you want me."

"Not that way." He took her into his arms to hold her as he watched her face. "You need to want me so badly that you'll ask me to love you."

"Oh, Clint..." There wasn't anything else she could say. Looking up at him, she leaned against him, reaching her hands to his head. As she absently arranged his hair to match her watercolor, she said, "My life was so easy before you came here."

"I was an innocent bystander. I saw you, and that was all it took. You lured me with a testing of your new contact."

"I didn't mean to lure you."

"You had no choice. We were fated to meet, and we'll be together the rest of our lives. And as soon as you realize that, my life will be a whole lot easier."

She frowned at him. When had he begun to look so drawn? So tired...so used? "Are you feeling all right?"

"I've been pushing it so I can have tomorrow afternoon and evening free to hold your hand."

"Honestly, I'll be okay."

"Don't you want me there?"

"Oh, yes! Of course! But not if you have to exhaust yourself."

He directed: "Kiss me as sweetly as you know how."

He was so dear. She was barefoot again, so she had to stretch up on tiptoe. Therefore she slid up his body an inch or two, in order to reach his lips with her own.

He could have helped her by bending just a little, but he didn't.

He was on the edge of madness with wanting her, and that slight sliding of her body was sweet torture he couldn't resist. His hands moved without his permission, but he controlled their greediness. His hands treasured her, touching, palming. Then he took control of her gentle kiss and deepened it with great shuddering restraint, bending her back over his arm and running his free hand up her side to smooth it over her breast, to caress her there.

She gasped, and his kiss became something she'd never experienced. It was almost as if she was... frightened? Of *Clint*? She trembled and her hands went to his chest to push—but they didn't. They just rested there.

Lying back, supported by his strong arm, she felt faint. Her heart was pounding furiously, her breath came in shallow little gasps, her knees had dissolved, and quiverings shimmered low inside her stomach in a way that was very unsettling. Her hand became so heavy that it fell from his chest to hang idle. After that she didn't notice anything but his kiss. *This* was a kiss. It was the kind you saw on the screen. It was what she'd always craved; what she thought she'd never experience. This was magic. This—

He lifted his head. His face was flushed, his whole body was trembling. With sweat beginning, his breathing had become ragged. His eyes were blue flames as he looked at her, lying back on his arm. His hand still lay on her soft breast.

She was lax, her eyelids almost closed. Her face was pale, her lips parted. She was boneless. She'd fainted? What had he done to her? She frowned and opened her eyes a little, and he knew he'd ruined everything. He'd been so patient, and with one starving kiss, he'd wrecked everything. All his plotting was shot to hell.

She lifted her head somewhat on her fragile neck, and her frown deepened. Forming the words with some effort, she was hostile: "Why did you have to quit?"

The shock of her words went jolting through him! She *wanted* his kiss? *That* kind of kiss? And under his hand, he felt her nipple hardening. As if scalded, he let go of her, then steadied her. He gulped air. He thrust his hands into his trouser pockets and looked at the ceiling. Then he went stiffly over and tried to lift the bookcase. After that he walked around until finally he could look at her.

She was standing like an abandoned marionette at an odd angle, with her hands holding her head on and her eyes staring out the window.

"Are you all right?" he asked cautiously.

"How can I tell?"

He went to her carefully, not really sure what to expect, and bent to look into her face.

Her pupils were enormous, and her face was serious.

"Are you going to do it again?"

He coughed and paced before he came to a stop beyond arm's length from her. "I want you to mark this day on your calendar," he lectured. "If ever, in all the rest of your entire life, you should doubt my love, you remember this day. If I didn't love you above my life, you would now be flat on your back on the floor, and I would be ravishing you."

She looked at him a long time. Then she almost whispered, "I'm...not...sure...it would have been...ravishment."

After a seemingly endless silence, he said foggily, "I believe we're making progress."

They stared at each other, then she smiled. She tried not to. He smiled back. She laughed, and he followed her laughter. They laughed until tears came—so joyously. And they fell into each other's arms. He lifted her to his chest and swung her around the almost empty studio, and their laughter was loud.

Mac came in from Ann's bedroom to see what was going on. He sat and watched with marked patience, waiting for them to realize they'd disturbed him. He was fully confident that they would then settle down and be quiet, so that he could go back to his nap.

When they had collapsed onto the floor, grinning at each other, Mac turned back to the bedroom.

Never even having seen the cat, the pair watched each other with fond smiles. With unpracticed coquetry, she asked, "Shall we?"

His body became intense with agreement, and his lips parted in anticipation. But a happenstance temptation wasn't in the plan. Regretfully he replied, "Not yet. Don't be impatient."

"You're a strange man."

"I'm the man who loves you."

Love wasn't one of those things that impressed Ann. With some irony she said, "I thought I loved Harry. I only loved the man that I thought he was. And what I'd dreamed he was slowly shredded away to nothing." That was what love did. It was an illusion.

Clint saw the disillusionment and he said gently, "That's why we're waiting. I want you to be sure."

"I'm afraid of love."

"It's something to be cautious about," he agreed. "You can get tangled up with a gypsy woman who casts spells with contacts."

She followed that line of thought with: "I never believed I really belonged to my parents. I know I was born to them, but I never felt as though I was actually...of them."

"I've read of people who feel that way."

"They are so baffled by me. I used to pray that I could be normal."

"You aren't abnormal, you're unique," his deep voice assured her tenderly.

"You're so kind to me."

"Do you realize that you love me?"

"I resist knowing. You're too disruptive. I'm uneasy."

"But not afraid?" he probed.

"That, too. Not of you, but for my peace."

"You can't live in a cocoon, wrapped snugly away from living."

"But I have my paintings and my backyard and Mac."

"No people?"

"Mary is my contact."

"Not I?"

Earnestly she told him, "I'm so tempted with you. But it's as if I must leap from the cliff into fog. I don't know where I'll land."

He moved his hand to touch the side of her head. "I would be there to catch you, to lead you through the fog and guide your steps until you can see."

She regarded him soberly, then turned her head and kissed his wrist before she shifted and folded her legs

Indian-fashion. "You should be in advertising instead of law. You have such a way with words. You need to be in some field that comforts people, helps them to understand."

"I'm in law for that reason. The language of law is complex. I believe in order and for the rules to be used as they were intended, not manipulated for greed or trickery or evasion."

"We need you in Washington."

"I'm not a politician."

"I suppose—" she drew out the word "—you could stay in your cocoon here in Indianapolis and never experience true testing and— No, no! I—"

But he had tumbled her and pinned her to the floor. She was laughing up at him, and his smile was very dangerous.

He warned, "Little mice don't mess around with big cats. Better give up belling me."

"This time." She tried not to laugh and caught her lower lip in her teeth.

He saw her do that, then he leaned his head down slowly and nibbled until she released her lip to his kiss, but he gently took her lower lip between his teeth and tugged it just a little before releasing it. Their eyes were open, and with a shudder, her breathing changed. His breathing roughened. He lifted his head enough so his eyes could focus better. Then he bent down and kissed her.

He curled her toes and shivered her nervous system. She raised her knees, and they shifted. Her hands groped and clutched in his hair.

He lifted his head and watched her face as his hand again sought her peaking breast. Then he leaned his head to it and suckled the lengthening nub through her shirt. She made throaty sounds and arched her back.

Abruptly he turned away to lie on his back, with one arm across his eyes. Abandoned, she looked at him with some indignation, then rolled up and moved over to him, to lie across his chest and push her head under his screening arm to kiss him. He allowed her to do that for a while, but then he set her aside and said, "I'm late." With that remark, he patted her hip and kissed her *forehead*. Then he rose to his feet and walked off, leaving her sitting there on the floor! He was whistling as he went out the door.

Ann slammed things around all afternoon. She went down to the gallery and was impatient and cross.

The way she acted startled everyone, but they were tolerant, attributing her conduct to nerves. Mary frowned at her.

Ann had *never* slammed things around, but she then directed two pictures to be moved and strode around looking at them before she had them returned to their original places.

Jon told Ann. "Go to the club and swim."

Mary told her quietly, but through her teeth, "Behave!"

And Ann became indignant.

She went home and flopped onto the swing in the yard, jerking the swing back and forth with impatient feet as she sat tensely rigid.

Then she jumped up, cleaned the pond and had to keep pushing Mac back away from the fish, who made themselves obnoxiously available. They couldn't be deliberately taunting the cat because fish were just...fish. Mac was willing to have the fish tease him.

With the pond clean and the fish intact, Ann replaced the grid. She then looked critically at the backyard and decided it was tacky. She began *weeding it*!

Clint found her there. He stopped to survey the bald patches that had appeared on the victimized yard, making it look very like an amateur's badly done haircut. Then he looked at Ann with a marvelously smug smile.

Seeing him, she knew it was *he* who had disrupted her paradise! She snarled, rose up on her knees and threw a clump of weeds at him—roots, dirt and all. He dodged her barrage easily, and he had the gall to laugh.

He went to her as she scrambled furiously away. He caught her effortlessly, picked her up and carried her to the clean pond, removed the grid, and ignoring her life-threatening shrieks, he dumped her in.

As Mac watched in fascination, Clint got into the pond with the woman, wrestled her still, and then kissed her. The kiss should have steamed the water from the pond and left the fish flopping helplessly. It didn't. It was probably the summer's high humidity that prevented that from happening. Mac was disappointed. He turned away to go inside to rest up for the evening.

Mac's harsh tongue had barely cleaned one side of his leg, when the man carried Mac's slave into the bedroom, dripping nasty water all over the floor, and he *put her on the bed*! In disgust that anyone would bring all that water onto his bed, Mac jumped down from it and left.

Clint looked down at Ann. She lifted her chin and sank back on one elbow. He took off his soggy suit coat and it splatted on the floor. He took off everything else, as she watched, closing her right eye to see perfectly, but finally opening both, mesmerized. He was beautiful.

Then he came to the bed, sat beside her, and quite efficiently began to peel her out of her soggy clothes. She resisted somewhat. He didn't notice. He took the top sheet and dried her off vigorously, then less so, then selectively. He kissed her water-cooled mouth.

How could she be so cooled from the pond when his flesh was still so hot? His arms pulled her cool body to his heat, and it felt delicious. She squirmed to get closer, and her breasts rubbed into his chest hair. Her hands went to pull his arms closer around her and then to his shoulders to try—impossibly—to get him closer yet.

He laid her on her back and stretched out beside her, half covering her. "Your time has come," he told her. She shivered. He advised, "Don't resist me."

"Go ahead." Her permission was as she'd always given it, except that this time she was impatient and a bit cross.

"When you ask nicely."

She pounded his back with her weak, quite ineffectual fists and shook her head furiously, as she almost cried. There were her broken breaths and tears; although she didn't actually cry, she was furious! However, when he tried to lift himself from her, to calm her, she wouldn't let him go.

It was then that he kissed her. He consumed her. He was so rigid as he lay on her. His hard hands and stiff fingers scooped her closer. His breathing was uncontrolled, his heart pounded and he was lost for several mad moments until his iron discipline reasserted itself.

That was what really caught Ann: that even now he could stop himself, for her sake. She began to relax. Again he had given her control of him. He would not take her until she wanted him. Suddenly she understood that she did want him. But it was still a giving—then.

She allowed him to do as he chose, but lying still, she again became tense. However, she couldn't stay that way. He didn't reach quite far enough as he turned her and slid his hand around her bottom, and she squirmed to help. Then he lifted his mouth, too soon, from her breast, and she had to put her hand on the back of his head to hold him to her.

And when he moved his sweaty face down her stomach, swirling his whiskered cheek gently over that sensitive flesh, she had to curl her body and lift her knees, as her breasts rose wantingly. Her hands clutched into the sheet and her head went back; her eyes closed and she made sounds in her throat that she heard, and thought they were exactly as she felt.

His hands were hot and his breath was scorching. His kisses were wet and seared into her flesh. He suckled and licked as he slowly drove her wild. She became frantic in a helpless way, not knowing what to do. She began to clutch at him. She wanted to touch him and kiss him in turn. She felt a need to taste him, and discreetly licked his shoulder and rubbed her teeth on his flesh as his fingers touched her.

She heard his sigh as she pressed against his fingers, but he took them away from her. She made a complaining sound. He chuckled with such a deep rumbling that it made a wave of sensation sweep through her body because it sounded as if he wanted to be there with her and was pleased that he was. His laugh was the most erotic thing she'd ever experienced. So far.

He put his hard palm flat against the most sensitive part of her core and rubbed, in one rather rough swirl, before he dragged that hand up and over her hip to reach around and touch her again.

"You could...go ahead." She had swallowed in the middle of her words. She was moving restlessly, pressing, touching, trying to breathe less noisily.

"When you ask me."

"Don't be an idiot."

"Say please." He had to gasp the words.

Their bodies were rather slippery from his sweat. They slithered erotically as they moved, and their hands slid on the other's body. He cupped her breast and gently squeezed, and she put her hand over his and pressed it closer, tighter. His eyes widened and darted to her face, but her eyes were closed and her small smile was ecstatic. She hadn't noticed what she'd just encouraged—no, demanded of him. He scrubbed his hand down her, more roughly, and she writhed in her pleasure. He said huskily, "Ask me."

"Please." She breathed the word urgently.

But he made her wait a little longer, for she'd tensed, braced. He lay on her, allowing her to feel him, and he kissed her yet again—softly, gently—and he touched her tenderly. She relaxed, and he lifted his head so that he could see her as he eased into her. She was surprised, and tensed again. But her clutching muscles didn't delay his entry; they closed around him, and she was startled. He held still. She relaxed, then clutched again. He groaned, and it was she who laughed.

"You gypsy witch."

"It's marvelous! It didn't hurt!" She moved. She experimented. She drove him crazy! His sweat dripped. He sounded as if he'd run miles. He felt that way, as if he'd never reach his goal. He clenched his teeth and counted. He did his damnedest and she wiggled and slithered and became frantic. Then she begged, "Oh, *Clint*! Help me!"

And he moved.

She clutched and strained, she clenched her teeth and struggled, she cried out and thrashed around. And she wept as he took her to the top, over the exquisite rim, and off into the magic realm.

# Five

---

As he lay sprawled beside Ann, Clint's breathing gradually calmed. With ponderous movements he turned onto his side and looked at her. Slowly he put a lightened hand on her stomach, for she still lay as he'd left her. In a chiding tone he said, "You promised me that you were frigid! What a lying gypsy trickster you are!"

She was watching him cautiously. She smiled a little but didn't reply. Then she carefully curled up to discreetly pull the pond-dampened sheet over her naked body.

He couldn't allow that. He took the sheet from her hands and flipped it back down to the bottom of the bed as he scolded, "What are you doing?"

"I thought you'd want me to cover up."

He stared. "Why?"

"He always...turned away and said...to cover myself."

Clint's expression was blank as he assimilated that. Then he said with restraint, "The poor fool." He watched her still face for a minute, then his own expression softened as his glance moved down her. He looked at her with great pleasure. He moved his hand on her stomach, then turned his head in a single shake, as he clicked his tongue once. "Frigid. Yeah. Sure. What a snare you set for me. A challenge?"

Timidly she lifted her hand as if to touch his face. She was so hesitant that the shy act caught his attention. He leaned his head to meet her hand and kissed it. Then he ducked under it so that her hand was on his nape, and he leaned forward farther in order to kiss her very sweetly.

She whispered, "I was frigid."

"Never." He grinned at her. "I'm glad you tore up the yard before I got here. I tremble in my boots to think what might have happened to me if I'd gotten here at the height of your running amok. Thank God you expended some of your energy on the poor weeds before you hit me."

"I missed."

He gestured widely to indicate his condition. "Only with the dirt. What a vixen gypsy wench! I'd like to see you dance, now that you realize the scope of your emotional communication. Man, can you communicate! Wow!"

"You threw me in the pond." She felt called upon to mention that.

"No, I didn't!" He was indignantly defensive. "All I did was dunk you, to cool you, on this sticky summer day. You were so hot—" he was wickedly smug

"—that you didn't realize what you needed—first—
was a rinse off."

She gave him a patient look.

"I got in with you." He acted as if that made him
acceptable.

"You drove me crazy."

"That's only fair. You've had me out of my mind
for almost two months!"

"Do you mean that I'm not anxious about tomorrow's opening? That it's you who's been upsetting
me?" She peered at him through the single contact.

"Not I, my one-eyed gypsy. Only you have been
upsetting you. And me, as a sideline."

She opened her right eye and stared at him. "I've
never felt anything so boggling in all my life. I lost
control."

He cleared his throat. "Uh...we ought to do it
again, right away." He tried to look earnest. "When
one tries something new, it's best to practice the skill,
so one is sure not to lose the touch." He took her idle
hand and put it on the back of his neck. When her
hand just stayed there, he reached back again and
moved it up into his hair. Then he took her other hand
and rubbed it on his chest and down his stomach.

"I'm still recovering," she stated sturdily.

"By the time you're recovered, I might be interested again. The last words I recall, you were begging
me to help you, so I suppose you'll require my involvement yet again." He smiled like a Cheshire cat.
"I'm always willing to help a lady in distress, but if
you should have another such attack of lust, I have to
be ready for you. You need to begin working on me
now, to attract my attention."

"I'm quite calm."

"Stick around. You'll change."

"Don't do that."

"Why not?"

"You...we won't do it again for several days and—"

He smiled salaciously. "Let's lay a little money on this. How about twenty cents?"

Her interest quickened. "Do you mean that you would want to again? Tomorrow?"

"Honey, since you've opened the gates—of your willingness—we could well be at each other all night long. You'll probably not even show up for the opening...of your show at the gallery tomorrow night." He kissed her longer and touched her here and there. Light touchings, which indicated his interest, in order to call her attention to the fact.

"I...don't think..." She quit even trying to speak.

He lifted his head from her moistened tummy button. "What don't you think?" he asked with bright-eyed interest.

"I'm not sure."

"Don't worry about a thing. I believe I'll be fully prepared for another attack whenever you're ready."

"You're feeling pretty cocky, aren't you."

He laughed immoderately.

She gave a long, patient sigh, but then she grinned for a while before she began to laugh. "How amazing it was."

"Yes."

"I never dreamed it could really be that way. I thought people lied."

He looked at her quite tenderly. "Poor Harry. Look what he missed."

"I'm not sure he enjoyed me that much. I was so frigid, he would turn away as soon as he was done."

Clint heard the "as soon as he was done." And she'd thought it was all her fault? That she was the underlying problem of that marriage?

Sadly she admitted, "I wasn't only frigid, I'm a poor housekeeper. I'm not neat and tidy."

"He married you to keep his house? He couldn't tidy up? He couldn't afford help?"

She studied Clint. He was indeed a different man. Her own parents had said she was the cause of Harry's anger. They'd said no wonder he got mad at her. She was a terrible housekeeper. "I was a poor housekeeper."

"You sat home twiddling your thumbs all day?"

"I was Harry Warsaw's wife. I was suddenly on every committee you can imagine. At twenty, I was snatched into and hurried along in a stream of people who were older than I, who knew what they were doing, and who assumed I did, too. There were meetings, luncheons and . . . madness! There were cocktail parties and dinners. There were faces and names and I was expected to adjust. It was my job."

"Since it was your job, he didn't think you needed any help? He runs his business all by himself?"

"Yes," she agreed. "Really. He runs the corporation alone. He doesn't allow anyone else to get a hand in."

"Then he'd come home and supper wouldn't be ready?"

"Oh, yes, I love to cook, but I hated cleaning up. There was never any time, and the house wouldn't be tidy."

"All I ask is that occasionally we change the sheets."

She watched him warily. "I won't move in with you."

"I want to marry you."

"No."

"If you think I plan to be an occasional stud for your awakened appetites, you underestimate my sense of possession." He narrowed his eyes at her.

"I'm my own woman."

"You also are mine."

"Now, Clint—"

"Good, it so happens I'm in the same frame of body. Mine is ready. How nice you are—"

"I'm not 'your woman.'"

He confirmed it: "My one-eyed gypsy woman." He moved above her.

She was indignant. "I didn't mean—"

But he had lowered his chest and moved it to rub away her protesting hands, from between them. His face was interested, amused and sure. Then, with skill, he simply rubbed his wily sex into her body, and she gasped. He eased down, pressing deeper, trapping her weakly defending hands with his chest. How interesting. How different was this man.

While she gave a fair defense, she wasn't rigid. She was feisty. She did frown, but she didn't hurt him, and at the last minute, she pulled her hands free from their entrapment and said, with some sass, "I'm not ready!"

She hadn't said not to make love to her or to leave her alone; she'd just said she wasn't ready. So he lifted his body and braced himself on his hands as he dipped

into her heat and swirled around nicely. "Not...
ready?"

She slid a look at him. Pertly she formed her lips
into saying "No."

He lay on her, deeply embedded, cradled her head
between his big hands and almost kissed her. But not
quite. He moved his face around hers, not quite
touching her, but his hot breath roamed, and there
were the sounds he made as he breathed, licked his
lips, moved his tongue and swallowed. He sounded so
hungry! Like a beast about to devour his prey. Her
chest lifted and her breasts tautened. Her hips arched.
Her fingers dug into the sheet on either side of her,
and she drew in a long, shaking breath. He smiled into
her eyes. She had to look a little cross-eyed to see him,
and the blue depths disoriented her.

He asked, "Want a kiss?"

She watched him. How rude of him to let her be the
trigger of his passion. He was ready. He didn't need a
kiss. He was asking her. She lowered her eyelids
halfway. "A little one."

His kiss curled her toenails. She felt it happen. She'd
never be able to wear high heels again. She forgot her
toenails and drowned in the "little" kiss. Her hands
came up from the bed and clutched on to him. Her
knees drew up and her heels locked together behind
him. How had they known to do that?

He moved with an insidious slowness. She wanted
to hurry upward, toward that remarkable summit. She
urged with her breath and body and sounds. He was
in no rush. She twisted and writhed. He paused. She
tried every way she knew, in her recently acquired box
of tricks, to excite him into frenzy. But he wouldn't
respond to her urging. Then she realized he was being

deliberately slow. She collapsed back onto the bed and released her greedy arms and legs to lie flat under him. This was another kind of torment?

It was. But it wasn't to punish; it was to pleasure her. It was a courting of her senses. What had been surface need as he drove deep into her core became aching want. It wasn't simply a coupling, it was a mating.

He moved slowly, but not too much—just enough to keep her at that pitch. He turned her and took her, slanting his body at different angles. He tasted her, his hands began to know her with more familiarity, his body learned the sweetness of hers, and his mouth the taste of her. It was just fortunate that she'd given him the first release, so that he could last.

Ann had never dreamed that making love could be such a sensual feast. Her own hands moved timidly and her mouth took sips of him. She wasn't bold enough yet, but she needed to feel and taste in turn. It was amazing to her. And the feelings he aroused deep in her body were shimmers of ecstasy. But those feelings spread to every cell, to every nerve, as the thrills slid over her surfaces.

Her sighs were music to his ears—the sighs of passion. His hands shook with tremors as he touched her, and his body shivered with his renewed need. She was delicious to his hands as he carefully touched her, squeezed her, rubbed her marvelous flesh. His tongue hungered for her and found the various tastes of her.

He separated from her so that he had more freedom in arranging her to suit him as he explored her. With her little gasps and the beginnings of her writhing, he became so hot that for his sanity's sake, he had to couple with her, pushing into her hot sheath. And the doing of that almost ruined his slow dance. It was exquisite torture to lie on her, embedded in her, and not rush to completion.

How long he'd yearned to be just so. To possess her. Or was it he who was possessed? He really didn't care which, just so that he was there, with her, his starving sex where it wanted to be, fully inside this woman.

But it wasn't only a fusing of their bodies; it was a mingling of their spirits, of their essence. He touched and moved and intoxicated her. He was very skilled. As he had played the violin, he now played her. He melted the last of her frozen core into a pulsating fire of desire.

Every nerve she had was tingling with awareness. Her brain swooned with sensation. Her hands moved almost in a ritual of encouragement, giving pleasure as she took it. It was beyond her knowledge that she moved so wantonly. She gasped through the small shocks and shivered with her muscles' impulsive grasp of him, and so did he. Their dance of passion was slow and sinuous as they were carried back into that realm seldom visited by mortals. The spiralling vortex dissipated at the zenith, flinging them far away, briefly, into another time.

They moaned sighs of repletion and panted with their slow return to reality. Their slick hands still moved on sweaty bodies and each aftershock was nearly painfully sweet. Finally their exhausted bodies, tired arms and laboring lungs relaxed, and they lay quietly.

He struggled to slant his heavier body from hers, but they stayed coupled. Their eyes were closed. They were spent. He said gruffly, "I love you, Ann."

"Yes."

"Marry me."

She was silent for a long time, then she slowly shook her head.

He opened his eyes and studied her pale, drawn face. "Are you all right?"

Her eyes stayed closed. She smiled faintly and laid her hand on his possessive arm still resting over her body. She moved her palm in a tiny, gentle swirl of a caress.

He risked it: "Then you want me to leave you?"

She frowned over the words. Then her eyes popped open and she gave him an indignant glare. "No!"

The frowning glare and the word soaked into his roughened ego, healing it, and gave him a satisfied smile. "Then just what do you intend doing about me?"

"I'll . . . use you."

"What a crass thing you are! What about me? Do you think I just want to be a sex object to your lustful body?"

"Don't you?"

"Well . . . yes, but I want more."

"Not tonight."

"You sure got to be a smug, sassy woman fast!"

"I met a man." She gave meaning to the last word. She looked at him and smiled a wickedly feminine smile. Then she moved her head over and set her opened mouth on the front of his shoulder. She touched her tongue to his salty flesh and kissed it—a wide, wet, sucking kiss.

He moved back above her, but their kisses were those of contentment, a sharing of another kind of love. He finally moved from her to lie beside her, holding her hand, smoothing her hair back from her face. "I should have taken you to a glade for this first encounter of love."

"Why?"

"For my gypsy to revel in her natural body reactions to love in a natural place."

"Bedding a gypsy in a bed isn't natural?"

"Not for you. You appear so cool and aloof, and you're a caldron of fire. I wanted you the first time I saw you, there at the cocktail party at the offices. You stunned me. I had to have you. But I had no idea it would be this way."

"Neither did I. I didn't know anyone ever had such experiences."

"It wasn't an 'experience,' Ann. It was love."

"Yes."

"And you'll marry me."

"No. I'll be your lover."

"Why only that?"

She explained softly, "It's all I can give. I can't marry again. I must have my freedom."

"You would have it with me."

"You'd want me committed to you."

He nodded in minute movements to show accepting understanding. "As I would be to you."

"No. You would have your life, and me to come home to. I need my own life, under my own control. I can't let go again."

He assured her, "I'd have no objection to your painting. You have great talent, and it would be wrong not to use it. I wouldn't put you in a tower, isolated."

"There are all kinds of towers."

"You can't secede from the human race."

"Yes, I can. I have. This is the way I want my life. I was perfectly content until you forced your way into my small world. I've accepted that you are a part of it. I can only adjust to that much."

"But there's the whole rest of living!" he protested.

"I've had it. I never want it again. I'm safe here."

"What, in God's name, did he do to you?"

She replied simply, "He cured me of marriage."

"And a great deal more."

"He never gave me what you've given me tonight, Clint. This has been marvelous. Unbelievable. Thank you."

"We gave to each other. But we gave more than pleasure. We gave love."

"Yes," she agreed.

"I'm patient. You'll come to want our lives to meet, just as our bodies do."

"If that's what you expect, then we shouldn't see each other anymore. You'll only be miserable. This is all you can have."

"We'll see." He took her into his arms, close, and held her.

"I'm sure. Don't badger me," she warned.

"I'll wait."

"It would be futile."

"No."

"I've said so." Her words were quick.

"You said you were frigid," he reminded her unfairly.

"You're a different man."

He took that up: "There. You've said it all."

"I cannot be as you want me to be. Believe me in this: I will *not* give up my life."

"I only ask that you share it."

"You ask a great deal more than that. I've told you I'll share love, but that's all."

He thought about that for a while before he asked, "May I stay the night?"

"I would like that. I suppose this is one of those times you'll suggest clean sheets?" She was even a little teasing.

"I'd go sleep in the weeds with you." His words were serious. A promise.

"That shows how much you'd bend—now." There was cynicism in her words.

He demurred. "That shows how much I love you and how far I would go to please you."

Again she said the word: "Now."

"We'll take it a day at a time."

They changed the sheets, showered, and went to bed to sleep in each other's arms, to waken in the night, surprised to find themselves together; to be awed by the raging need so quickly roused and which could be slaked so deliciously.

With the morning, they wakened to smile and yawn. They touched each other, still amazed. He asked, "Will the time come when we accept that we're together in the morning?"

She cautioned, "We aren't going to live together."

He sobered. "No?"

"There could be times, like this, when you stay overnight, but it won't be every night."

"Even when it gets cold and icy? You'd make me get up and go out in the snow and bitterly cold wintry night and go home?"

"Or I will." She hurried him. "We have to get organized. Today's the opening. Good Lord, look at your suit!" It was just where he'd shed it last night, and it lay there, still in a damp heap. "I'll put it in the dryer on Fluff, and see if you can at least wear the trousers. What a rash, mad man you are," she scolded. "You get into the pond in your clothes!"

"You did."

As she left the bed she turned and stood, naked and glorious. Her black hair was a tumbled cloud around her head as she looked back over her bare shoulder. "If you recall," she told him, "you dropped me into the pond."

"Yes. But I didn't just leave you there. I did join you."

"Join me? I wasn't coming apart!"

Ahh, he thought. But she had been. She'd been furious with him! Tearing up the clumps of weeds and hurling them at him. But now she was making a little joke with him. What would she have been like if she'd never known Harry Warsaw? A natural woman. Could she become one still? What would it take?

He rose from the bed equally unclothed, and with a small smile, she watched him come to her. He said, "Coming apart? I probably should check your connections."

She laughed, and it was some time before they again got up from the bed to shower and do something about the day.


Ann was serene before the opening. Mary and Jon were amazed that the catamount from the day before apparently had no qualms about the show. With composure and organization, she worked as she had the year before. Clint was there, and he called the firm and requested Dingus McGee to come help.

Dingus did come, but he wasn't at all sure gallery openings were on his agenda of office duties, or that he wasn't playing hooky. So it was a while before he settled down, accepted that he was actually free to enjoy this unusual experience, and gave his whole attention to doing whatever was asked of him. Clint duly noted all of it.

In the late afternoon, the workers parted to dress. Mary was so excited about the evening that she'd brought her clothes to Ann's, to dress there.

Handily blocked from going home with Ann, Clint just smiled at his love. He said, "I'll fetch you ladies in plenty of time."

Ann still couldn't actually kiss Clint in front of her sister, Mary, but she smiled at him almost as if they were alone, and she touched his arm without realizing she did that. With a communicating glance at Mary, he grinned, left and went on to his apartment.

An Opening of a Show at a Gallery was an Occasion, so why not dress for it? Why not, indeed. So they did.

Ann wore a slim, black, floor-length gown, high necked with a plunging back. But as she moved, tiny pleats opened in the skirt, below her knees, and scarlet flashes winked. She wore black heels, and her hair was up in its severe knot. Scarlet hoops were in her ears, and she wore a bit more makeup for evening.

Mary despaired of looking anywhere nearly as dramatic as Ann, so she simply looked smashing. Her gown was a glitter of blues, slender and lovely; and in her ears she wore Ann's elegant shoulder-touching rhinestones. She sparkled under any circumstances; now she had reason.

Both men came to Ann's house, and they were dressed formally. After working all afternoon, Dingus had requested permission to attend, and in Ann's studio, they wrote him an elaborate invitation with curlicues on vellum. He kept it.

Dingus wore his summer tux with the casualness of familiarity, but Clint looked as if formal dress had been created just for him. Clint took Ann's breath. He'd probably have taken Mary's, too, if she'd noticed him; but her stare was locked on Dingus. She told Dingus, "You cleaned up fairly well."

He nodded, not really hearing what she'd said. He told her, "You look like a film star." Dingus kept a little distance from her so that he had the space needed in order to simply look at her, which he did in some awe.

Ann and Mary knew all the people who came to the opening, and their guests were introduced to Clint and Dingus.

Clint watched as people were greeted by Ann. She smiled but was a bit aloof. It was the guests who reacted. They liked her. They were pleased to have received her invitation, and they really looked at the pictures.

Sharon's catered marvels were her usual genius, and the opening was a great party. Ann's parents came early with several of their friends. They were very nice people who viewed Ann's paintings with their usual wonder, and they smiled at Clint kindly.

Clint had noted that the prices on Ann's pictures were far too low. Almost all of them were sold in the first two hours. And there were guests who asked for appointments. While Ann demurred to some, saying her schedule was too full, to others she agreed rather offhandedly and said to contact her later.

It wasn't until almost ten that Harry Warsaw came in with a group. Ann looked at him blankly, with no response, astonished that he'd be there. Clint put a hand at the small of her back and moved nearer so that his chest touched her arm and she would know that he was there.

Harry leaned and kissed Ann's pale, cold cheek in a hearty way and said jocularly, "So you've found a hobby!"

How like him to negate her talent.

Then Harry looked at the man who loomed protectively. "Clint Burrows, isn't it? I'd heard you'd moved here. Why here?"

"Warsaw." Clint acknowledged only the name. He gave Dingus a hard look.

That astute man approached the new arrivals. "Come this way. Would you like some wine?" And the group moved on. As Harry passed through the crowd, there was the slightest breath of a progressing gasp, and as Harry moved on through the gallery, a following wave of chatter and laughter came over the crowd. Harry was a power and very acceptable, so he was greeted and people talked to him. He and his entourage perfunctorily viewed the paintings as they sipped their wine, but Clint saw to it that Ann was unavailable when Harry's group left.

Clint found that Ann's hands were cold and shaking, and she seemed in a daze. He asked her, his voice low, "Are you all right?"

"Yes. I wonder how he knew?"

"No invitation?"

"Surely you can't believe he'd be sent one?"

"It did seem improbable."

"The last time I saw Harry Warsaw was in a truck stop in Oklahoma."

Clint waited, but she turned away, making it clear she didn't want to speak of her ex-husband.

Clint followed. "We could move anywhere in the world you would want to name."

She lifted her glance to him. "I could love you."

"You already do, my fool."

"I'm not a fool, I'm a gypsy."

The corners of his eyes crinkled. "I like your mother and father, those sane people who've had to cope with the awesome changeling dropped into their crib. I wonder what happened to the ordinary child they actually had?"

"Ordinary like Mary?"

He acknowledged that problem with a nod as he speculated: "Your parents must feel they've been the victims of a quirky fate. They seem such mild, nice people. Mary would knock them off-center all by herself, for she's an exceptional woman, but they got you, too! How they must have looked at each other. Do you suppose your father thought your mother had been fooling around in the woods with a satyr?"

"She'd never do that."

"Still waters run deep."

"She doesn't even swim."

"That's the most prosaic thing you've said in two months."

"I'm not sure I want you to know my parents well. That part of my life is safe. It's similar to the safety of my own world. You've invaded my space, and I'm uneasy for you to come to know all of my other segments—of friends, interests and my parents. It makes you too much a part of all the portions of my life."

Reasonably and quietly he told her, "I am your life, as you're mine."

"No."

"Who shall we invite to our after-show party?"

She stared at him. "We're having a party?"

"Oh, yes."

"Where?"

"You'll see."

# Six

As Ann stood and looked around the room at those present, Clint's glances at her were those of a conquering male. He warned her: "You're not to close your right eye in order to use that left contact. I've been in a tussle with a gypsy witch who's depleted my strength to such a measure that if some man challenged me, I'd be hard put to defend my property."

"Property?"

"Uh...position. I knew it started with a *p*." He looked innocent. But then he growled, "Don't go testing that contact."

She protested, "But it's fascinating to see the colors—those in the paintings and those on the women. Men dress in quite a marvelous counterpoint to women. Accents to the colors, like sherbet cleansing the palate."

"I hadn't realized that's all we were good for—as plain accents to the colors in a crowd of women."

"We need to have some reason to keep you around."

"Just don't wink. I don't want to have to wrestle any man for your favors tonight. I have other plans."

"Oh? And what are those?"

"I'll let you know after our party later on."

"Oh, yes, the 'party.' You want me to do a charcoal drawing of the opening for you?"

"Not tonight. Who do you want to come to the party?"

"I don't know. I'll ask Mary."

So it was Mary who chose the handful of couples who would attend the after-show party. Again it was impressed on Clint's awareness that Ann really didn't pay much attention to friends. And from the conduct of the people there, it was by her own choice. They were willing to be closer; it was Ann who stayed aloof.

The selection of the guests by Mary was added proof of Ann's conscious choice of isolation. What woman had Clint ever known who hadn't been excited about a party, jumped into the planning and invited the guests? None. Only Ann. She wasn't even really interested in the prospect of an extension to the evening's festivities. She didn't need people.

Clint narrowed his eyes as he looked around at the gallery's cheerful guests who milled and visited and laughed. It was stimulating to him to be among them, and he realized that Ann only endured the gathering, waiting for it to end.

Clint liked people. Was Ann's aloofness a temporary thing, caused by being thrown into the maelstrom of activities, too young, as Harry's bride? Or was this a character trait that couldn't be changed? Would it be a problem?

Clint was a gregarious man. Could he survive in the isolated, insulated world that Ann had created? He'd spent time and energy to achieve the recognition he now had in the field of law. He took pride in being consulted, in the respect his name carried, in the monetary return. But there was more to life than being king of the mountain.

He wanted more—a home to share, friends with whom he could be close. He'd chosen this particular firm so that he could live in Indianapolis, to know all that it offered, as a town of a million people. It was big enough to suit sophisticated tastes, but it had all of the advantages of a middle-sized city. So there he was, where he wanted to be in his thirty-sixth year. And he'd fallen irretrievably in love with a reclusive woman?

If she were genuinely reclusive, these people would be more withdrawn from her. People don't turn to those who are deliberate loners. There has to be some response. The people there were completely at ease in their attitude toward Ann. She could have all the friends she wanted.

Alone, she was missing too much in losing the pleasure of casual friends. He would change her.

He smiled like a benefactor ready to do his share in the expansion of her life. He'd changed her sex life, at great personal strain. Every tortured minute had been worth it. She was more than he'd ever dreamed. If his effort could bring about another such release into friendship, he was ready.

Whatever it took, Clint decided, he would change her social life. If he could relegate business to business hours, she could adjust to friends. He was going to widen and enrich her life. The after-hours party was a start.

As the other guests left, the selected couples were told to linger. The few were quite delighted to be chosen and became so animated that the party seemed to continue longer than usual. It had been a great opening.

Ann was her usual cool self. Clint would look at her possessively and smile, for he was so amused by her. Who else knew she was a wildly sexual being? If the emotion shown in her paintings was discounted, only he knew what a wanton she could be. He was thrilled that that was so.

As was always the case when Sharon catered, there were no leftovers; but at Clint's direction, she had reserved two boxes of the delicious morsels. Sharon kissed Ann's cheek and said it was a marvelous party, and she said again how much she loved Ann's watercolor of her son.

Jon told them not to worry about the debris in the gallery. It would be cleaned by the night crew. He, too, kissed Ann's cheek and congratulated her. It was obvious he valued her.

So the residue of guests left the gallery and found their cars. When Ann was alone in the car with Clint, she turned to him with the boxed hors d'oeuvres on her lap. "Your apartment?"

"No. Wait 'til you see."

"I hope they don't stay. I'm quite tired, what with one thing and another." She smiled at him.

He laughed out loud and reached to take her hand and put it on his thigh.

She lifted her nose and said primly, "I was speaking of the show."

"And me spending last night trying to sate your lusts."

"Clint, you are outrageous!"

"You were magnificent tonight. You were magnificent last night, too. But I'm very proud of you, Ann. Your paintings are superb."

"I've been told I should choose a particular subject and stick to it, in order to make a name for myself in that medium and subject."

"Do you want to?"

"No."

"Then do it your way. You're unbelievable."

"I could probably make more money if I worked to become a fad."

"Do what you enjoy."

"I knew a man who did paintings of Amish buggies for seven yea—" She was looking around and realized where they were. "Are we going by my place first?"

"Yes." He pulled into her drive.

"Oh. Well, perhaps I'll change. I have a new pair of—" She had stepped from the car. Then she turned to him, as he came to her. Blankly she said, "The other cars are here."

"Come see." He was so pleased with himself. He took the boxes from her and indicated that she should go up the steps to the porch.

She hesitated as she asked, "What have you done to me?"

Her voice was so soft that he didn't listen to her words. "You're in for a surprise."

"I'm already shocked."

He unlocked her door and stepped back with a big smile. With the others crowding in and exclaiming, Clint watched her face to share her delight.

With a chilling stillness, Ann saw that someone had been there before them. There were several large palms placed perfectly around her studio. With them there, the room was pulled together into an entity that was a showcase. The painting-filled walls, the artist's accoutrements of easels, pots of brushes and tubes of paints carelessly scattered on the painting tables—even the abused floor—looked elegant and stylized. It was exciting to the eye, well-done.

And in her pleasure of sight, Ann's mind appreciated it all. But, unbidden, someone had been in her sanctuary.

Talking among themselves, exclaiming, the others moved inside as Clint told Ann, "There's more." He tugged her arm and urged her toward the north-wall's tall French doors, which led outside.

Her backyard was a fairyland. There were tubs of flowers in the bare spots left by her frenzied attack on the yard the day before. And around the pond were lighted candles.

The candles were in myriad heights in an imaginative arrangement of holders. They were fairy lights. The view of the lighted yard was breathtaking. With the tumble of weeds and flowers, the carefully selected tubs of daisies and begonias, and the grid-covered pond, it was simply beautiful. But Ann's eyes saw not only that it was lovely and perfectly done; she saw the intruders into her world. And it was Clint who'd had the key to her private kingdom, and he who had allowed the others to come in. She felt betrayed.

How could he claim to love her when he knew her so little? He knew her not at all. He was a stranger. He was a disruptive alien. She'd made a very serious mistake.

So had he. He stood beside her, used to her silences. He was so pleased. "The florist did an excellent job of it, didn't she? Sharon suggested her."

Their guests came from the house with exclamations of pleasure. They went along the walks, which had been designated by candles set in sand-weighted paper bags. Soon one couple was in the tree-hung porch swing, and one woman was being swung by her escort in the rope swing. They had made themselves at home. Shoes came off, their talk was soft, and laughter sounded often.

Mary came and slid her warm hand around Ann's icy-cold one. Mary didn't say anything. She was simply there. She hadn't known about this plan or she would have stopped it. Mary had assumed they were going to Clint's apartment. Clint had wanted to surprise Ann. He had succeeded.

The guests looked around Ann's studio and looked out over the yard with shining eyes. They said variations of: "I would expect your house to be this unique." "You aren't the ordinary woman." "You're wonderful to share it all." And, "Clint said it was to be a surprise. Were you surprised?"

And she replied with quite honest horror, "Yes."

Clint laughed in satisfaction. It had all been worth the effort. He kissed her cheek and was concerned to find her skin so chilled. He frowned and touched her shoulder, then her hand. "You're freezing! Where can I find you a wrap?"

"I'll get it."

She passed Mac coming from the bedroom, and the cat looked at her for some explanation, but she went on by. She took two aspirins and faced the fact that she would have to endure. There was no way she could demand they all get out of her place. Her place. Hers.

"Honey, are you all right?" Clint was there.

"You're just like Harry." She went past him to the hall closet and took a heavy woolen sweater from it.

He was stunned. "What? What do you mean?"

"After he had sex, he would pick a quarrel, too. I should have expected it."

"What?" He was appalled. "What do you mean?"

"You've succeeded."

He reached out for her arm, but she jerked away and went on outside to... her guests.

The next two hours lasted several weeks. Her guests had the most marvelous time. They loved her backyard. Under the cat's patient, proprietary stare, they took turns swinging. They strolled the candle-lighted brick walks, they removed the grid, and with lifted skirts and rolled-up trousers, sat on the edge of the pond with their feet in the water.

Being a formal man, Dingus didn't wade. He was seated with Mary in lawn chairs by the pond. Mary was very quiet.

Dingus asked her, "Are you feeling unwell?"

"I'm fine."

"Sleepy?"

"No."

Dingus observed, "Not your usual chatty self."

"No."

"Come sit on the swing, and I'll sing to you." The prospect of rash conduct amused him.

"I need to see if Ann needs me."

Dingus countered, "Clint's taking good care of her."

"He invited all these people into her sanctuary."

Dingus wasn't dumb. "Uh-oh."

"He didn't understand," Mary told him.

Dingus admitted, "I was surprised when we came here."

"Then you realize he's blundered?"

Dingus shook his head once in sympathy. "I'm almost as private as Ann."

"But your privacy is training, while hers is retreat."

"Ahh."

"And of all nights, Harry Warsaw chose tonight to come to her opening, and all it did was to remind her what it was like to be a public personage, and it reinforced her retreat."

"Will she be all right?"

"She isn't paranoid, just private. Had Clint waited a while and asked beforehand, she might have adjusted to it. Why do people insist on surprises?"

"They generally mean well."

"But then you have something like tonight. Clint meant well, but he probably set their relationship back to zero. Why are macho, outgoing men attracted to shrinking violets?"

Dingus put one hand around her arm and shook it one tiny shake. "Why are belles attracted to retiring men?"

"Are you talking about us?"

"Yes." He smiled a little.

"What makes you think I'm attracted to you?"

"I've seen to it."

"You're not my type at all." She lifted a prim nose.

"You'll adjust."

"For a 'retiring man,' that sounds extraordinarily macho and assertive."

"You affect me in that way."

She laughed, sparkling for him.

"Will Ann be all right?"

"It will depend on how Clint handles himself. How close they've been. If she loves him."

"They'll probably be okay," Dingus said as he watched the unsuspecting intruders, who were guests, bask in the strange yard's magic. With careful thought as to the revelation, Dingus added, "I believe he stayed here last night."

"Now, how can you know that?"

Dingus was a little uncomfortable. He didn't like to appear a gossip, but under the circumstances, he felt that Mary needed to know. "I have the apartment that overlooks his car space. His car wasn't there last night. He drove in this morning and his clothes were a mess. I asked him where he'd been. He said in Ann's pond, and he laughed like a man who's been...taken care of."

"How can you say this?"

"He implied it. And you had to've noticed how they were...together at the gallery this afternoon. After the way Ann acted yesterday, contrast that with the way she was today."

Mary was thoughtful. "Maybe they'll be all right."

"Not if she slams the gates."

Mary nodded. "To the castle."

"While this is charming—" he waved a hand to indicate the house and yard "—I'd hardly call it a castle."

"Dingus, you've a limited imagination."

"Expand me."

"I just might."

"You've already made an awesome beginning. I could use a little care."

"I . . . just . . . might consider it."

He coaxed, "Let's sit on the swing."

"Do you sing on key?"

"Not relentlessly."

Ann thought the guests would never leave. But finally they did straggle away, so reluctantly, and they all promised they'd be back. As they voiced their promises, Ann had her arms wrapped around herself, in that heavy sweater, so her appalled shivers weren't so noticeable. Several did note that she looked chilled, but attributed it to a residue of opening-night nerves. One said, "Sensitive people have such a hard time of it." And another agreed: "That's right. But if Ann weren't so sensitive, the paintings wouldn't be so marvelous." Still another exclaimed, "Aren't they?" There was the question, "Do I have to wait a whole month to get mine home?" And the chatter went on.

But there were two quiet people among the easy exchanges—Ann, who simply endured, and Clint who was very troubled. She'd flung that "You're just like Harry!" at him, and she'd not really spoken to him since. He badly needed some kind of explanation. Her feeling so cold wasn't natural on that hot and humid August night.

When the last of the guests had gone and there were just Mary, Dingus and Clint, Ann said, "I'm sure you'll all excuse me. It's been a long day, and I'm completely exhausted. Good night." As she turned away, she gave Mary the quick wink that begged her help.

Mary took it up immediately. "Let's go." She efficiently tried to herd the two men, but neither was really herdable. Dingus said, "The candles have to be extinguished."

And Clint added, "The grid has to be replaced."

But Ann said, "You have a key. Lock up after yourselves." And she turned away. She hadn't the strength to spend the time it would take for Clint to understand that they were through. She couldn't endure another man using her life so casually. Another man who deliberately quarreled with her after sex. A man who used her briefly, when and how he chose. Never again.

She locked the door to her room and even pitched Mac out the window. He didn't mind. He could go around and see what damage had been done to his secret lairs. It was the time of night when everything was still, and he could prowl as if the world were his.

The last three people took a while to leave. Ann could hear the murmur of Mary's stern voice. She was committed to getting them all away. Bless Mary.

Ann stripped and got into bed. But last night's sheets smelled deliciously of Clint. The scent of him distressed her in a way that gave her agonies of regret. She had thought he was different. No one had ever mentioned that all men were this way. Why would a man regret sex? Regret it to the point that he provoked a quarrel to "wipe out" the memory of his having been intimate with a woman?

She took his pillow and held it as if it were he. And she wept.

He was there. He tried her bedroom door. He growled, "Open this door this minute. I have to be with you."

She was silent, her sobs muffled by his pillow whose fragrance was of the man.

"Ann, I command you to open this door, for our sakes. I don't know what I've done." And again he said, "I have to be with you."

She made no sound. As she had been that first night, she was silent.

She heard his steps leave the hall, and she knew as he moved soundlessly in the tangled yard. He came to the window and simply slit the screen, unlatched the catch, opened the barrier and climbed into the room. She lay in the dark with saucerlike eyes as he undressed and came to her bed. She whispered, "No."

"Yes." His voice was so gentle. "Whatever the quarrels in our lives, we will still be together." He got into her bed, took her cold, stiff, resisting body into his arms and settled her there. "If you'd rather not talk now, we have all the rest of our lives to resolve whatever it is that bothers you. I'll listen. And there's the chance I'll add a word or two, here or there. But you're so cold and tired, perhaps this should wait for morning. Let me get you warm."

She shivered. She knew he would make love with her, and she would respond, but she didn't want that intimacy. Not now. How could she be firm with a man who hadn't allowed a locked room to deter him? She braced herself.

But all he did was to draw her cold, shivering body against his heat. He placed himself so that she was spooned against him, and her frozen feet were warmed along his hairy legs, her cold bottom was tucked against his furnace lap, her frigid spine was nestled against his hot hairy chest, and her icy fingers were covered by his big, square, warm hand. He said, "I love you. Just you keep that firmly in your mind."

As her shivers subsided and her body calmed and warmed, she said, "Any other man would have had sense enough to've stayed away from me."

"I'm not any other man. Even you have admitted I'm different. I love you, Ann. We can work out anything that comes along."

"I'm not that strong."

"You have me. You don't have to do anything alone. I'm here."

She lay thinking of that; and still thinking, she went to sleep. He didn't sleep for a long time. But even when he finally did, he knew every time she sighed or moved.


It was late Saturday when they wakened. She was suddenly conscious that she wasn't alone, and she opened her eyes as she heard his broken breathing. A nightmare? He was in distress. Her instant compassion caused her to lift her head from his arm to look at his face, and she found him awake with his blue eyes watching her.

"What is it?" she whispered.

He smiled ruefully. "I'm somewhat disturbed to be lying naked in a naked lady's bed."

She blushed and would have moved away from him, but he held her there. "Good morning, lady."

"Good morning."

"Is your castle completely bricked up this morning?"

She knew that he realized something was very wrong, but she wasn't sure how to explain it to him. How did one explain the male to a man? How could she, when she didn't understand them either?

"Why did you accuse me of being like Harry last night? What was this about having sex and then quarreling deliberately?"

"He would do that. After he was finished with me, he would be silent for a time, then he would begin to pick a quarrel. I'm not a type who likes quarreling, so I would placate him. It only drove him to more determination—even if it took days. He would push with hateful words and unwarranted criticism, until I'd finally get mad. Then it was as if that satisfied him. It was strange."

"How could you equate that with me? I didn't quarrel with you."

"You brought all those people to my sanctuary. You used your key to bring in people to change it."

"Oh, my love, I meant only to please you."

"By an invasion of my world?"

"I didn't mean for it to be an…intrusion into your world. I thought of it as our world. I wanted to share it with your friends. I love you so much that I wanted them to have some of our happiness. I wanted to decorate you with gems and rings and golden things. I wanted to fill your house with flowers. How could I have been so clumsy as to annoy you?"

Now, how was she supposed to be annoyed with that? As obnoxious as he had been to invade her house, invite in other people and destroy her privacy, how could she object when he did it to share love?

She watched him for a long, irritated time. "I can see that you're going to be a trial to me all my life."

With those unkind words, she had admitted that he
would be around in order *to* be a trial; and he laughed.
He hugged her, blew loose lips into her neck as he
rubbed his whiskery face there, and his arms closed
around her with the usual masculine possessiveness.
She allowed that, too.

"You're like a sticker burr," she said ungraciously.

"I should shave?"

"Oh, no. I like whiskers. I'm just having a very hard
time shaking you off."

"Well, I will help you try. But in order for you to
shake me off, first I have to get on. Right?" So he
turned her flat and . . . got on.

"I don't understand a man like you. You appear
urbane and knowledgeable, but you seem quite incapable of understanding when you're not wanted."

He smiled and moved. "You want me."

"Being sexually tolerant and trying to get rid of
unwanted attention . . . Ahh."

"Yes?" He was asinine. "What sort of attentions
are unwanted? This?"

"Uh . . . that's okay."

"What about this? Hate this?"

"Uh . . . no."

"How about this?" He was heartless. "Shall I stop?
Or would you like me to do this?"

"Ye-e-es-s-s."

"About these 'unwanted attentions' . . ."

"Shut up."

"Did I hear *Ann Forbes* saying 'Shut up'? I can't
believe a lady like *Ann Forbes* would say such a crude
thing as 'Shut up'! Shocking."

"You want to be shocked? Try this!" And she
reached a sassy hand around and one finger tickled

him in a very intimate place. But the shock was physical, not social.

Their play became quite hilarious. They tumbled and laughed. He chased her outside and through the garden using the walks for a fox-and-goose game. With the fence so high, they were completely private. And they made love in the grasses—breathlessly laughing, teasingly incomplete.

Then, prolonging their play, they rinsed off in the pond. Sharing with the waterweeds and trying to catch the startled fishes who, until just the day before, had led quite a dull existence with only Mac the fraidycat to watch them.

Sitting in the chest-high water, Clint examined the marvelous beauty and grace of his love. "Who would ever believe that under your smooth facade is burlesque humor?"

Quite coolly she replied, "I'm a gypsy and easily led. I've come under a strange and disruptive influence just lately."

He shifted closer. "Is that right? Is this influence something that should concern me?"

"It *is* you!"

"My mother and father will never believe it. They know me for my diligence—" he reached out and cupped her breast "—my respect for the female gender." His thumb indicated that. "And my sober devotion to duty." He lifted her to his receptive lap.

"If you make love to me here in the pond, the fish could become addicted to sex and I could become inundated with fishes."

"I like the word *inundated*." He undulated.

She laughed, leaning her head back, her wet black hair hanging down her back, her hands on his shoulders. Then, sitting on him, she pushed back his hair and held his face in her hands. She leaned to kiss his mouth very sweetly. "I love the flowers. And the candles last night made this a fairyland."

"I wish to God I'd never done it. I was afraid I'd lost you, and I couldn't understand why."

"Don't bring anyone else here."

"I promise." How easily he said the words.

# Seven

Harry Warsaw phoned Ann that Saturday. "Well, hello, Ann," he said in his smooth way. "You're maturing quite nicely. You looked really beautiful last night. I want to see you again."

"No."

He laughed charmingly. "I, too, have matured. Let's have lunch next week. How about Wednesday? At our old place."

In sour irony she inquired, "What . . . 'old place'?"

"We used to go to Jeb's Attic, back in the old days. Don't you remember?"

She tried to recall ever having gone there with him. "No, Harry. I don't remember, and I don't want to see you again. It's finished. Let's leave it that way."

And in the exact, careful way that Clint had spoken to Ann when they first met, Harry coaxed, "We had a nice thing, Ann. You were just too young to adjust. Let's meet and talk."

"No. I have a guest. Goodbye."

"I'll call you next week, and we'll talk."

She simply hung up.

Even though he was standing three feet from her, Clint felt as if she was miles away. She wrapped her arms protectively around herself and shivered. He reached out and drew her to him, enclosing her in warm, sheltering arms. "Harry...Warsaw?"

She nodded against his shoulder.

Clint became a bit more tense, more alert, ready to man the barricades. "What'd he want?"

"I've matured, and he wants to talk."

"And does Ann Forbes want to talk to Harry Warsaw?"

"No."

Very carefully, Clint casually mentioned, "You said the last time you saw him was in a truck shop in Oklahoma. What happened?" And he held his breath.

Ann couldn't remember mentioning Oklahoma. Her thoughts on that other time, she released herself from Clint almost absentmindedly. But then she took his hand, and they walked out of the house into the backyard and to the swing.

As they went along, Ann told about the quarrel. "He was picking the after-sex quarrel. And he'd been pushing me—verbally. At the truck stop, I'd been served an unordered bowl of carrots. I didn't want them and put the bowl over by his place.

"He shoved the bowl back at me and said through his teeth that if he'd wanted carrots, he'd have ordered them. I said I hadn't ordered them either, and I'd just thought that he might like them.

"I realize that this sounds ridiculous, but it is typical of the beginning-quarrels that he used to cause me to rebel. At the truck stop, he then went on to say other things—critical things. He was a little loud. His voice carried to the tables around us. I was embarrassed and very shocked. He was generally selective in where he quarreled with me. Perhaps being in a strange place—the truck stop—he felt no one would know us there. I don't know what he thought. He was really rude.

"By then I had suspected Harry had a problem that had nothing to do with me." Her speech was a little agitated. "I couldn't say anything, I didn't look around at all, I knew people were listening and I was ashamed. We sat there at the table, and Harry ate his meal as if he was alone.

"After a while, a couple stopped by our table. They were, oh, forty or so. The man was bucktoothed and freckled. He wore a farm cap, worn jeans and a plaid shirt with the sleeves rolled up. His wife had a relaxed body, her hair was frizzed, and she had solemn blue eyes. She, too, was in jeans and a plaid shirt. The man said to me, 'You want to stay here, or would you like to go with us?'

"It had never occurred to me to just walk out. I had been raised to be obedient; Harry was older than I, and a figure of authority. I had been so sure that I could change our lives and make the marriage work. Marriage was for life.

"But after two years, I'd had enough of Harry. I didn't care about anything. I got up and walked out. The couple had expected trouble, because they'd paid their tab. So we just walked out, got into their big truck and drove off. Such a simple thing to do. But I was *free*!

"It was very brave of the Bateses—Jim and Fran. They could have had no idea what a mean-mouthed man would do, but they risked it to help me. Fran is the sweetest woman, and Jim's as gallant as any knight. We hardly said a word. When we came near the Dallas-Fort Worth complex, they asked if I'd like to go any special place. They knew truckers who went everywhere, and they said they could help me get wherever I wanted to go. I asked where they were going, and they were a part of an old hippie commune out in west Texas. I went along.

"They called the place Peace. The name labels it for the time it was formed. To look at the Bateses, you'd never have believed they were such a radical pair. And yet they're still radical. Who else would have rescued me?"

"I would have."

She touched Clint's knee and smiled. "The commune is a neat, busy, organized community now. They truck-farm exotic fruits and vegetables, design and make exquisite rugs and elegant pottery, and make posh soft luggage. They've sorted themselves out into permanent couples, and the kids have settled with their own mothers. They are as middle-class as any little town, but they still have that sixties independence. That 'Wait a minute, let's look closer at this' kind of strong, patriotic, individualism of the sixties. It was a spine-straightening, look-'em-in-the eye experience for me.

"I worked. I did what I could do. I'd been in my second year at the Herron School of Art. I can draw. So I did designs. I did my share of whatever needed doing, like loading trucks in the morning with the vegetables to take into Austin, or pack luggage to ship. Whatever. Everyone was very kind. *Tolerant* is probably a better word for them. They expect you to do your share. And if you're also pleasant, that's a plus.

"There was one totally irascible man there whom everyone walked around, but as long as he didn't harm anyone or speak unkindly, they allowed him to stay. There were other strays. I've never been involved in such a...family. My parents never quite seemed to quit looking at me in surprise. Do you understand? They love me. Very much. But they never...quite understood me."

Clint allowed himself a sympathetic "Yes."

"Fran was the one who decided I should go back to school. She wanted a wider scope for me than rug designs and tourist watercolors. I was contented with what I was doing there, but she said why not do the best I could?

"For such a comfortable, maternal-looking woman, she has the mind of a steel trap, and she's an encourager. She's a 'why-not-er.' She is a woman you'd want in your life, if you're unsure."

Rather forlornly, Ann then mourned, "But I think she pushed me out of the nest too soon. I didn't learn enough from her."

Clint suggested, "Maybe she just didn't realize she was passing you from her protection to the protection and discipline of study. How long since you graduated? Two years?" He watched Ann's nod of agreement. "Give yourself some time. I'd like to meet them."

Ann nodded to show she agreed with his words. "She'd have you running for president."

"Maybe I'd recruit her into running one of the corporate headquarters I represent."

"Ahh." Ann laughed and shook her head. "That would be something to see—the two of you, sizing each other up and deciding how each could best be used by the country. She has everyone in that community working full-out. Not exhausting, physical labor, but stretching their minds and talents. It's exciting.

"At school I did a portrait of them. I painted Jim sitting on a stone outcropping that was like a primitive throne, with Fran standing beside him. Jim's look is steady, calm, in control. And Fran is looking out of the picture to assess the viewer. My prof said I had the 'touch.' That was his word. I thought I'd pleased him with the rendering, but I overheard him tell another professor that I should be a name in a hundred years, if I could continue to share what I see." Ann's head was down, looking at her fingers, and she looked up at Clint. "What I painted wasn't in me—it was the Bateses. I simply copied them. But how many Jims and Frans does an artist find?"

"Could I see the painting?" He rose from the swing.

"I took it down to Texas and gave it to them. I couldn't send it. I had to be there to explain it so that they would understand. I'd painted them in their trucking clothes. It's what they wear. The accoutrements of civilization aren't important to them. But it is a portrait, and I worried that they might take it wrong.

"Without any explanation at all, they understood it. Fran cried. Jim said, 'Even the clay.' He *knew*! He is a strong, good man, and God made man from clay."

Ann shook her head and wiped her eyes with quick fingers. "It was the most thrilling thing that had ever happened to me. Up until then." She added that very shyly and didn't quite look at him.

He didn't misunderstand. He sat back down, put his hand on her nape and shook her head a little. "When the prof said you would be recognized in a hundred years, he meant widely cherished. You're recognized now." Then he added what he'd been wanting to say, "You sell your things too cheaply."

"I'm just glad people like my work. I know a writer who would write for nothing, just to share her stories. I'm like that."

"Fran would tear her hair."

Ann laughed. "You understand her exactly."

"We must be kin."

"She would have reared up and her eyes would have flashed, if she had been here when Harry called. I've never talked about Harry to anyone but you, actually. I was at the commune for almost a year when the divorce was granted.

"Mary came down like a visitor from another planet, and the people stopped work to stare as she walked through the community. She's like a dream, so blond and beautiful. She and Fran were instant friends. With such diverse facades, they're a lot alike. Mary is more protective."

"I've noticed."

"Why didn't you let Mary run you off last night?"

"I had to be with you."

"You do weasel your way in."

"I love you. I need to talk to Fran about you. I need her advice."

"Why?"

"I'm even more protective than Mary. I need to know how to balance my urgent need for protecting, while allowing you your need for freedom."

"Then you understand."

"Yes."

She was silent, thinking. Then she said, "How lucky I was that day in Oklahoma. I wonder if I would ever have left Harry, if I would have just endured. How awful to think of a whole life of...endurance."

Clint warned her, "He came last night to check you out. He's been hearing about you since your last show and came to look you over. He saw all those vital, young, upwardly mobile adults. He saw a young, talented, gorgeous ex-wife who was a part of that, and he wants in. He's a clever businessman."

"Is that why you're hanging around? You want in?"

"Good thinking."

But he didn't make love with her. He held her and he kissed her, but he was careful. He had become a little unsure with her. He'd found she could close him out. After last night, he realized he couldn't just decide what to do about her and do it; he'd have to be cautious. It was a new experience for him.

The next time, after Harry called Ann, Clint went to see him and told him to back off. That did finish the nuisance of Harry, and he didn't call her again.

As the days went by, Clint and Ann were together in their summer idyll. Ann danced for Clint in that tangled Eden as he played his violin. She moved to his impassioned music, and his eyes feasted on her as his magic sounds floated away on the summer air. They were lovers. And once, as he lay replete, she took her tempera paints and meticulously decorated his flesh with imaginary flowers, enhancing his beautiful body as if for pagan worship. Then all that talent was smeared by her heated body, and was washed away among the startled fishes, along with his fleeting regret.

Their lovemaking never seemed to be the same. It was new each time, and it was delicious. How could that be? Part A fit into part B, and they moved as in C. But sometimes they were serious, and sometimes there was a poignancy that lent a marvelous timelessness to their love. Sometimes they rollicked hilariously, and sometimes they made fast, quick love—hot and wild. It was wonderful.

And they talked. They argued about religion, politics, football teams and world trade. They were stimulatingly never on the same side.

But they saw very few people.

Clint had a hard time with that. He loved Ann and wanted to be with her, but he missed the stimulation of other minds. Ann's mind was creative, but his could follow hers only so far, and she was indifferent to the quirks and nuances of clever people who found themselves in court. He needed competitive minds.

Dingus was allowed into Ann's sanctuary with Mary, and that saved Clint from outward restlessness. The two men became good friends. But Dingus didn't challenge Clint; it was Clint who drew Dingus along. And while they could share, it wasn't enough for Clint.

Clint was at Ann's for dinner one night, and they were standing in the kitchen, shelling and eating their shrimp among the pots and pans, before taking their plates out by the pond. He began casually. "There are some people you should meet," he told her. "I need to repay invitations. I've ignored too many people, and I plan to make my home here, so I'm giving a party in my apartment in two weeks. Will you come? I believe you've served on a committee with one of the women."

Ann gave him a withdrawing look. "I'm beginning a new painting. I'm not sure—"

"You have to eat. You could come for a little while. Sharon's doing the meal."

Ann smiled. "That's the hook that gets me there."

"I wonder if I could afford to hire her for all the meals. Would you move in then?"

"That's fighting dirty."

"I'd really prefer to attract you myself, and not have to depend on food to lure you in. That cripples my self-image."

She closed her right eye and surveyed him intimately. "Your image is intact."

"Flirt."

"I believe I shall get a monocle. Then I could look people over in an intimidating way."

He assured her, "You're intimidating just standing still, doing nothing."

"Baloney."

"If you hadn't been testing your contact that day, I'd never have had the courage to approach you. I thought you had flirted impulsively and then turned shy."

"I am shy," she confirmed.

He corrected, "You aren't interested in other people. You aren't shy as much as you're protective of your isolation."

"I'm not isolated. I'm free."

"But you live in this world."

"I think I'll go back to Texas."

"No." He gave her no room for argument.

"I only want to live my own life."

"But you're enclosing me in your cocoon."

"You're free to break out." She watched him, wide eyed, not breathing.

"I love you."

"Oh, Clint." She put her arms around him and kissed him.

They stood there in that untidy kitchen, their arms holding each other. They didn't speak for a long time. Then Clint said, "I once read about a couple in a wagon train going to California. In the middle of an endless prairie, their only child died, a little boy, and he was buried there. The wife couldn't leave his grave. She asked how could she leave her child out there, all alone, in the midst of nowhere? And her husband hadn't the heart to force her to leave. He stayed with her, the wagon train went on, and they were left behind—alone. I would do that for you. I am doing that for you. If I must, I'll share your cocoon."

Ann raised her wet gaze to her lover's. "I was never meant to share a life."

"Don't kid yourself. You'll share mine." His voice was hoarse with his own emotion.

"I'll try." She meant it. And she did try.

Perhaps if she'd begun in committee work and social meetings under conditions divorced from Harry

Warsaw, she could have managed Clint's dinners more easily. As it was, she had to force herself each time. She sat listening, appearing calm and serene. But she counted the minutes until she could leave.

While she was in silent despair, Clint was proud of her. Could she live her life to suit him? His dinner parties were all catered by Sharon. They were perfect. Ann was simply another guest, and Clint was the perfect host. But everyone knew, by then, that she and Clint were a pair. The guests treated her as his hostess, and the invitations to him included her.

Then one night Clint had three clients to dinner. Their businesses had been merged successfully, with all parties feeling as if each had the better deal. Clint had been involved in the negotiations, and the clients were enormously pleased. It was a celebration meal several weeks before the Labor Day weekend. Sharon had outdone herself.

Ann was there. The words spoken were English but the meanings were foreign to the artist. Golden parachutes and White Knights and Shark Repellents meant odd things to her imagination.

The other three women talked designer clothes and compared experiences of trips to South America and various fat farms. With some self-amusement, Ann mentioned Peace, Texas, and hit an astonishing response!

The woman knew its products quite well! They were very curious and interested, questioning Ann closely about the town, and particularly, if there was any chance of getting the marvelous products at a cut rate?

There was none. The women sat there, in their glittering jewels with perfectly fitted gowns on their carefully monitored bodies, and shared groans of grief that they'd have to continue to pay full price. The incident would have made a succinct *New Yorker* cartoon.

"Ann Forbes." One woman frowned carefully at Ann. "You're the young woman who had a show at Jon's gallery?"

Ann nodded.

"You're quite...good. I know so little about art other than what I learned of the Masters in school. I have no idea how to judge it, but I was impressed. *I* liked what I saw. Do you ever do portraits?"

"Very rarely."

"I might like something little. Oh, perhaps a pencil sketch or maybe just a little watercolor. I'll call you."

Having sold most of her paintings by then, and feeling secure, Ann replied, "I'm already working on next year's show and have very little time. I do know several artists who do portraits. I'll give you their names."

"Oh, but I wouldn't want to go to a stranger!"

How curious. What was Ann to these women? They knew Clint's reputation and wanted a portrait by his mistress?

Ann stood by Clint as the guests said good-night and left, and by then the women had assured themselves that Ann would make an exception and do portraits of them. Just something little, of course; nothing too expensive.

Ann murmured, again, of other artists who were excellent at portraiture. But they finally left, the door was closed, and the couple was alone—at last.

"A good evening," Clint said. He was pleased. "How were the women? Apparently you made a big impression. Will you do their portraits? This could bring good commissions."

"No. They're looking for bargains. And I couldn't endure to paint them. They're plastic." She paused thoughtfully. "Of all the committee meetings and dinners I attended as Mrs. Harry Warsaw, these are the first truly idle women I've met. Almost all women are somehow involved with something: business, charity or families. It was an amazing thing tonight to listen to their conversation. You talk about me being isolated! They truly are. They really believe they're *in* the world. No, that they *are* the world. The only one tonight I'd paint was Judith. I could do her, but it wouldn't be what anyone would want to have. It would show her as lost as she is. Why do older men marry such young girls?"

He replied quite honestly, "A great many men can't cope with a confident woman who has a career and other interests. Most men want a woman with whom he comes first. We don't change easily."

"I'm a career woman."

"There are extenuating circumstances."

"As in?"

"You bend to me. You take me as I come. You include me. You're concerned for me. You're trying to change your life for me. I know how bored you were tonight. It was palpable."

"Surely not."

He shook his head and grinned. "You smother yawns brilliantly."

"A talent? But unmarketable."

"The State Department could use you. You can make the most boring entity appear to fascinate you. Thank God you didn't examine any of the men with your contact."

"I'm not wearing it."

"I have you—" he gasped "—in the raw?"

"Totally unadorned."

He surveyed her gown. "Not totally."

She kept her eyes on him as she kicked off her heels. Moving, deliberately so, she slowly reached back to unzip her long gown. She made a big deal of allowing it to ve-e-ery gradually slide down her shoulders to be caught on her peaked nipples. But leaning back just a trifle, she could pretend to earnestly jiggle the gown free, but she really only jiggled.

He moved back against the wall, as if in tolerance of her delay. He casually folded his arms across his wide chest as he watched intently. His head bowed just a little so that he looked at her from beneath his brows, and he pulled his lower lip between his teeth.

Ann gave up "trying" to dislodge the material from her nipples. But she had to stay leaning back from her waist in order to keep the dress precariously in place. She raised her arms and released the pins that held her hair so formally. One by one she discarded the pins, dropping them to the floor.

"My cleaning lady will wonder when she finds those pins."

Ann agreed but explained, "She'll write a *True Confessions* story and make her fortune."

He guessed, "She'll say they were her pins?"

"Undoubtedly."

"My reputation is shot."

She dismissed that : "It was ruined long ago in a pond on College Street."

"You've already written your own version?"

"I had to write it on asbestos."

He was shocked, "I thought asbestos had been outlawed."

"They understood the circumstances and allowed me to use it, just this once."

"When do I get to read it?"

"I can't risk exposing you to the asbestos. Instead, I'll demonstrate."

He shook his head once and lifted one hand to his forehead as his voice rasped, "You're tearing me apart. Half of me wants to take a giant step and rip off that gown, and the other half wants to be teased. You're driving me a little crazy."

"Good. That's the whole idea."

"You want me crazy?"

"Out of control. The way I feel."

"I like the way you feel."

She lowered her eyelids and smiled. Then with the hazardous position of the dress firmly in mind, she slowly shook out her cloud of black, gypsy hair. "Want me to dance for you?"

"My God. Would you?"

"Play for me."

"I can't. I don't want to be distracted by an instrument. I have a recording." He moved quickly from the wall, took her into rough hands and kissed her rather violently. Then he set her from him, and went into his living room. His fingers scrambled through the tapes and he finally said, "I could be quicker, if I could concentrate."

Her laugh was unfair.

"If you want to dance for me, don't laugh that way."

"Yes, sir."

"Or speak. Be perfectly still."

There was no reply, and he slowly turned a danger-ous, smoldering look over his shoulder. His eyes stayed on her like a hawk's on a mouse. Then he went back to hunt for the elusive tape. He slammed it into the delicate machine and punched buttons too hard. He turned to her, ripping off his tie and shrugging out of his jacket. He whipped off his belt and discarded it as he sat on the sofa. The music began.

It was truly gypsy music. It was a throbbing, sexually thrilling rhythm that wound around and teased. And that was what Ann did. She wound around and she teased. She was exquisite. She was sensual. She was a promising temptress, as she finally allowed the caught material to drop from those peaks. Then her hips delayed the gown's descent as she swirled them in lazy circles. But she had to stand in one place because the falling gown had puddled the material around her feet. Trapped, she stood half dressed, with the throbbing music urging surrender.

He couldn't last. He rose from the sofa and snatched her to him to bend her back and capture her soft lips with his demanding mouth. She was limp; he was master. He stripped off the tormenting gown, and she wore just the slightest red lace barrier. It was soon gone. He lifted her and carried her to his room.

He, too, was exquisitely sensual. He laid her down on the bed and bent over her, and his eyes flamed. His rough hands were stiff but oddly gentle because they were so harshly controlled. He stood, his breathing roughened, his eyes glued to her, as he took enough time to unbutton his shirt and take off his clothes. Then he came to her.

He explored minutely as if he'd never before seen a woman and needed to satisfy his curiosity. He licked and suckled, touched and pushed and squeezed. He kissed. When she would have done the same to his body, he captured her hands above her head and kept them there. So she moved in tiny writhings. She drove him wild. She made slight sounds and soft gasps that filled him with excitement.

His face was taut with desire, the sexual sweat filmed him, and he took her with care, then with strong thrusts, to pause, to rest, to build her excitement again. And he spent a long time making love to her.

She stayed that night. And it was she who wakened and sought clothing. But she could wear his. He smiled to see her in his big shirt, and nothing else. They made love on the living-room floor. They coupled and rolled and laughed. Then there were only the sounds of love. It was lovemaking of another kind. And they couldn't get enough of each other. Would they ever? Could the time of indifference ever come to such love?

# Eight

When the phone rang at Clint's apartment, Ann didn't touch it. Clint laughed at her reticence. "Too early for you to be a discreet visitor?"

She snubbed him. "I wasn't casually raised."

As he spoke into the phone—"Clint Burrows"—he watched her with wickedly sparkling eyes.

Ann half listened to his words, but she was bemused by the man. Clint's was a strong, masculine voice. He had only said his name, but from the way it sounded, whatever the problem was, he could handle it.

His side of the conversation was revealing. "Hello, Natalie, everything okay?" He listened. "I see." "I would love to have them." "No, I understand. You should go, too. I'll handle it. When do they get here?" "Fine. Tell the girls I'm looking forward to seeing them again." "Right." "I'll be here." "Bye." He cradled the phone and said, "My nieces are coming for a visit."

"Oh?" she asked with polite interest. "When?"

"Next week. Early on Monday morning."

"How long will they be with you?"

"Until Sunday. Sam, Natalie's husband, has a business appointment in Cincinnati, so they'll drive over from St. Louis, leave the kids here, and go on to the meeting, then stay the weekend. It's a chance for them to have a holiday together." Clint squinted his eyes as he said, "There have to be sitter services in Indianapolis. Know any?"

Ann knew nothing about anything connected with children. The only thing she'd ever done was to illustrate some children's books for a new publishing house that had soon folded. That was the extent of her contact with children. It obviously didn't qualify her as any source of information. She was so out of touch with the real world that she didn't even know any young mothers to call. And Mary didn't have an— "Mary might know something about this."

"Would you ask her? And I'll inquire at the office. There must be people working there who have children and have thoroughly investigated the sitter problem." He smiled at Ann. "They're good kids."

Ann thought it would be interesting to see his nieces. Would they be anything like Clint? It didn't occur to her to hustle around trying to solve his problem, or even to suggest that she keep the children during business hours. She drifted into his kitchen and made perfect crepes for their lunch, leaving a disorderly wake behind her.

Later Clint cleaned it up, as Ann sat on a high stool and read aloud from a cookbook while he absent-mindedly filled the dishwasher.

"What are you thinking?" she inquired.

"That we'll have a dishwasher and a housekeeper."

"You are assuming that I'll move in?"

"I'm assuming marriage."

"I've tried it," she reminded him. "And it's not for me."

"You tried the wrong man."

"You're right, there. But men are men." She shrugged, dismissing the subject.

"Right after we met, you agreed I'm different."

Emphatically she confirmed it: "You are marvelous."

"You're just talking sex. Any skilled man can please a woman. What about the rest of me?"

"You're really very nice." She closed her right eye and gave him a salacious appraisal.

"'Nice,' sounds wishy-washy. I want something more solid. Something like... Well, I suppose we'll have to invent some word good enough to describe me with you, as a man with a woman—and not in bed."

"What's wrong with being in bed?" she challenged.

"Or on the floor?"

"Or in the pond?"

"Or the weeds?"

"You're a madman, Clinton Burrows."

"For you." He kissed her. Then he put soap into the dishwasher and started it, before he lifted her off the stool and carried her toward the bedroom.

"I can't believe you want to make love yet again."

"In just about a week, I'll have two nieces here, and our free time will be sharply limited for almost *seven* days! Just think about that, Ann Forbes."

"Horrors!"

"See? One makes hay while the sun shines."

She couldn't resist pointing out: "It's raining."

"Not inside. We'll put on the ceiling light and pretend that's the warm sunshine."

"I love the rain when it's cool like this in August, with the first hint of fall. It was so hot the night before last that I was out in the backyard at midnight. High up were the honks and calls of the migrating birds. Already! I couldn't see any of them, but they've already started south. The year is dying."

That didn't bother him. "Another will begin."

"I love you, Clint."

"Marry me."

"Nonsense."

"How could any woman, in this day and age, say 'Nonsense' when a man asks her to marry him? Haven't you read any of the articles about the surplus of women? Men are scarce! You need to snatch this opportunity. You need—"

"I've had more than my share, with Harry."

Still holding her, Clint was frowning down at her. She returned his stare with a lifted chin and one leg straightened out as if to balance herself, or perhaps to show she wasn't really just lying there, docile and supine. Clint said, "Harry didn't count. I'm your share."

She smiled just a little. "You're more than enough for any woman."

That made him appear indignant. "You want a co-wife? You'd *share* me?"

"I'd take the . . . more intimate aspects of the marriage, and she could do the nitty-gritty."

He grinned. "So you like the intimate aspects of me?"

"I'd like to bottle and sell you."

"What exactly would you keep?"

"The whole of you. I'd only sell the essence."

"Want a little essence now?"

"I suppose I could tolerate a touch."

He laid her on the bed. "Where, exactly, would you like the . . . touch?"

"The portions of the conversation you choose to target fascinate me."

"I'll show you 'target.'" But it took him a long time in the doing of it. She mentioned the length of time, and he replied that was because she was such a slow learner.

"I'm not the one who is inspecting you."

"Oh. You noticed my curiosity?"

"When you turned me around like that, and bent me that way, why wouldn't I notice?"

"What would you like to do to me?"

So she showed him, and he was shocked. He covered himself with his hands and protested, making her almost helpless with laughter.

It was another way of loving.

When it was evening and Ann could emerge from his condo with some dignity, dressed again in her last night's evening wear, he took her home. But then he spent the night there.

And all that next week, he excused his sleeping with her by reminding her that the week after that, early on Monday, his nieces would be his guests. Therefore his time with Ann would be limited.

"I believe you're just using that as a handy excuse," she accused.

"I'll show you 'handy,'" he promised, and he advanced her knowledge in the meanings of words, which led to the study of parts.

She knew she would miss him that next week when his nieces were visiting; he was so sweet to her.


He called her at 4:22 a.m. the next Monday, and not only the hour warned her, but his voice was terse. "Honey, I have trouble. I'm over in Terre Haute. There's been a wreck. My brother-in-law, Sam, may make it. My sister's badly hurt. They're being flown to Methodist Hospital by helicopter. They're taking the kids in, too. The girls are okay but in shock. Could you go to the hospital and see about them?"

"Should I bring them here?"

"Wait until I get there. Then they'll know I know who you are, and where they are. If we aren't careful as we move them around, they might think they've been abandoned or kidnapped. This has been bad for them. They're upset. We should be there in about an hour. I'm leaving my car here and I've chartered a plane."

"Could I meet you at the airport?"

"I've called Dingus. He'll be there. There's work I have to delegate to him. I'll alert the hospital to watch for you."

"Is Natalie . . ."

"Very, very bad."

"Oh, Clint."

"Yes. Go to the hospital right away, so you can be there for the girls, please."

"I'll be there," Ann promised.

They hung up, but Ann immediately called Mary, who sleepily answered the phone with: "What's the matter?"

"How did you know?"

Foggily, Mary said the obvious: "Look at the time. Are you okay?"

So Ann explained what was going on and ended up saying, "I don't know what to do."

"Get dressed. I'll be there in twenty minutes." But Mary was there in eighteen. There wasn't such traffic that early, even in Indianapolis. "Bring some paper and crayons," Mary suggested. "We don't know how long we'll have to wait. How old are these kids?"

"I've forgotten." Ann was distracted. "Not babies. Around six? Somewhere in there."

"Were they hurt?"

"Shaken up. Their parents are hurt. Their mother's very, very bad. Those poor kids. What will we do with them?" She sought to share the responsibility.

Mary replied an automatic "We'll see."

So, as usual, Mary took over. They drove to the hospital and were directed where to wait. The personnel were kind and kept them informed. "The helicopters have arrived. The parents are in emergency care. The children will be examined, of course. Do they know you?"

"No. I'm a friend of their uncle's."

The nurse checked a clipboard. "His name?"

Ann replied, "Clinton Burrows."

"Yes. He's coming by charter."

"Yes."

"When he gets here, I'll tell him you're here." She turned to Mary. "Are you a relative?"

"Here." Mary indicated Ann.

The nurse looked at Ann, then back to Mary and nodded. "Can you stay?" But she asked that of Mary.

Mary replied her usual "Of course."

"Good." The nurse's voice showed approval. "You'd better have breakfast. There's time." She directed the sisters how to get to the cafeteria. "If Mr. Burrows comes in the meantime, I'll tell him where you are."

"There's nothing we can do for the children?" It was Mary's question.

"We're trying to keep their lives as simple as possible right now. We need at least twenty-four hours to be sure they're both all right. One nurse has been assigned to them and will stay with them until their uncle comes."

Finally Ann asked, "And Mrs. Durbin? Will she make it?"

"We'll try our best."


Ann and Mary sat and waited. Hospitals were places to wait. To wait to see someone, to be operated on, to be evaluated, to recover, to get better, to go home. Or maybe not any of those things.

Clint Burrows and Dingus McGee came striding in, bringing vitality and vibrant life with them. Ann watched as, without the turn of a hair, the very formal Dingus leaned and kissed Mary's mouth. He acted as if he had always kissed women in public. Ann was astonished over Mary and Dingus's kiss, even as Clint kissed her.

Ann really didn't relate to happenings, to current events, or to other people and their problems. Her attention had been weakly grasped while she studied the people in the waiting room. But she didn't study the people per se; instead her attention was captured by the light and shadow, the fleeting expressions that so revealed souls. She looked at it all as an artist. She saw life as an observer. Her feelings were locked away.

Much time passed—slowly, endlessly. Eventually a nurse came and said Mrs. Durbin still lived. She was now in intensive care. Mr. Burrows could see his sister for five minutes. His sister probably wouldn't know him. Clint looked briefly at Ann and went off.

It was the anguish that Mary and Dingus felt for Clint that attracted Ann's compassion. Clint seemed so strong. But after Clint left the room, Dingus groaned, put his elbows on his knees and his face into his hands.

Even then, Ann saw Dingus first as a troubled figure, beautifully proportioned, before she became aware of his concern for Clint. Then Ann saw as Mary put her hand on Dingus's shoulder in sympathetic support.

It wasn't until then that Ann's conscious thought accepted the gravity of reality. The situation was terrible. Clint was suffering. His sister was gravely hurt. Her husband was almost as bad. This was real.

And then there were the two little girls.... They shared about the same age difference as she and Mary.

Did the older care for the younger as Mary did for her? Then Ann really looked at Mary as a person.

This Mary was a stranger. This was the woman Ann had automatically turned to all her life, passing on her problems, accepting that they would be solved—that Mary would protect, shield, and give Ann care. And her sister had always been there to do just that: to respond and solve, to comfort.

Ann had always asked that of Mary. How amazing. Mary had never objected or gotten angry or refused. She accepted that Ann needed to be cared for by her. Mary had even gone down to Peace, Texas, and brought Ann back home. No matter what she'd asked of Mary, Mary had given it—time, emotion, support—every time.

Clint had called Ann to come to him, and what had she done? She'd called Mary. Not even Clint could ask for Ann's help. She just turned the whole problem over to Mary. And here was Mary, a rock, whose concern now included Dingus.

So even then, with her attention captured by the horrific drama, Ann only mused along over her dependence on her sister. Probably the only thing she'd ever done without Mary was to make the disastrous marriage to Harry Warsaw.

Mary had never forgiven herself for not realizing Harry was wrong for Ann. Even leaving Harry hadn't been Ann's idea. It had been the Bateses'. At twenty-six, Ann finally saw with clear eyes and understood that she was almost totally dependent on another person. That person wasn't the man she loved; it was her sister. And Ann accepted that it was so. She'd just never realized it before then.

Clint was back from his five minutes with Natalie. He was only somewhat visibly moved. His face was tense, and his movements were quickened, like those of a man warned of danger and girded to meet it. How could he battle death? He would try. "We discussed it with Sam, and he agreed we must tell Natalie that Sam was hurt, too. Sometimes that gives a person a stronger commitment to living for the sake of the children.

"We aren't sure she understood. I told her, since Sam's not too sharp. His jaws had to be wired together, and his face sewed up. I said the children were safe, and that I would care for them. Not to worry. Sam and Natalie are in the same cubicle. They're keeping them together. But he can't talk. He's holding her hand. I can see her for another five minutes in an hour. We'll let the kids go in, too."

"Is that wise?"

"They need to know what's happening. They're a part of this. They were with them when it happened. They wakened and saw. They know. They need to talk to their mother while she . . . still lives."

He said all that with firm communication, but a tear came from his eye and tracked down his cheek. He gave it no attention. It was like seeing a lion weep.

Dingus and Mary left for the office. There was nothing for them to do at the hospital. They would come back in the late afternoon.

Ann sat in the waiting room. She passed the time by sketching the people who also waited.

Clint paced between the five-minute visits. "I think she heard me this time. The kids go again this afternoon. Natalie's injuries are internal. They think she's

stabilized. Her face is the same but pale. Her eye-
lashes only fluttered this time. I don't know if it was
consciousness or spasms."

Ann said nothing.

Clint went on, "Thank God you're here. I don't
think I could stay glued together without you here
where I can see you." His eyes were bloodshot with
unshed tears. He leaned over, kissed Ann, then went
to wash his face.

Ann stared after him. He thought she was helping
him just by being there. How remarkable! She was his
strength? She? Ann Forbes? All she had done was sit
in the waiting room and draw faces for her sketch
book—marvelous faces. This was intensive care. The
faces of those waiting were unadorned with consciousness of self. They were all intently outside
themselves. They made interesting studies.

Clint and Ann went down to supper and Clint talked
about his sister and her husband, then about his family. His parents would get there the next day. His
brother from Florida and his sister in Chicago would
be arriving any minute. "I dread my parents having to
come. This will be hard for them. Natalie is their
baby."

Ann watched him, and when he quit talking, she
suggested, "Eat the fruit."

"I'll have some coffee."

She demurred, "No, the fruit will be better for you.
Eat it."

"I'm glad you're here. Did I tell you that?"

"Yes."

"Don't leave me."

His voice cracked just a bit, and it touched Ann. "I won't." But she wondered how he could draw strength from such a spineless person. Perhaps she appeared strong, since she wasn't really emotionally involved? She'd never met Natalie or Sam. They weren't real to her. The entire situation had the casual-seeming feel of familiarity. It was all so "known" from TV dramas: the crisis in the hospital, the agony of waiting, the recovery in the final scene. Dying wasn't in the script.

Clint's other sister, Sue, came from Chicago. She was caught up in a rush of arrival. She clung to Clint and barely acknowledged Ann in her quick talking to Clint. It was a pouring out of trivia, in her need to communicate reassurance. "I finally got someone to stay with the kids. Ned's out on the Coast, he won't come unless— He'll go on home and be with the kids. How are Cathie and Jan? Shall I go see them or will it just upset them? Poor Sam. So banged up and helpless to help his Natalie. Damn!"

With his family arriving, and being among them, Ann felt like a fifth wheel, but Clint locked his fingers around her arm and wouldn't allow her to leave. He was a pillar of strength for his sister; then his brother Rick arrived. He was older. Clint relinquished some of the burden to his brother. Ann was fascinated by Rick, who looked very much like an older, harder Clint. Rick looked Ann over and accepted her with a brief nod. Ann found she envied the parents this bulwark of strength. And she envied Natalie their love.

Only Mary loved her. And Clint? How much did he love her?

It wasn't until almost midnight when Clint took her home. He didn't stay. "You'll come in the morning?" he asked her.

"If you need me."

He held her in anguish and his voice grated, "You're keeping me going." He kissed her very sweetly. "I love you." Then he released her, and he went back to the hospital.

In the morning, his parents came to the hospital. Having seen the children, they were exactly as Ann expected them to be: strong, challenging death, defying it, sure they'd win. Ann wondered how it would be to have such strength, such support.

At noon, in the hospital cafeteria, she gave Mary a contact-lens survey and told her, "I've been letting you get away with a very sloppy moral-support program. The Burrows go all out, full tilt and hell to pay. You've been negligent."

Mary glanced up, distracted, and offered, "I resign."

"No, you can't. I just think you ought to study up and polish your talents. You can do better."

"How is Natalie?"

"No good. I get the two girls this afternoon. Want to come help? What does one do with children that age?"

"Wing it."

"Are you taking revenge for my critical evaluation?"

"No. I have a full-time job. I'm turning you over to Clint."

"He doesn't know beans about taking care of a woman." And even as she said it, she recognized it was a lie.

Mary shrugged and said the obvious: "Teach him."

"He thinks I'm giving him strength!"

"Believing that is half the battle. You believed I could do anything, and I did. But actually, I only rode shot gun. If you will review your life, you will realize you've done exactly as you pleased all along."

"But you always saved me," Ann protested.

"You gave me the feeling that I was needed, but I was always after the fact. Like in Texas. Fran and Jim had given you the opportunity to escape from Harry, and you seized it. If it hadn't been the Bateses, it would have been someone or something else.

"You had realized Harry wasn't for you, and you were already looking for a way out of the mess. They presented you with one, you took it and gave them the credit.

"I've known all along you never really needed me. I came to the hospital yesterday because I knew Dingus would be here. He's very loyal to Clint and he has a deep sympathetic compassion behind that stern facade. I needed to be sure he was all right."

Ann was astounded. "You'd choose Dingus over me?"

"Without batting an eyelash."

Really startled, Ann told her sister, "You shock me."

Mary scoffed, "You're stronger than you know."

"Only yesterday, I realized I'm totally dependent on you."

Mary smiled.

Ann declared, "I am."

Mary shook her head.

Clint came into the cafeteria and Mary rose and kissed his cheek. "Mother and Father would like your parents to come to our house. They'll be comfortable there."

"That's really hospitable of them," Clint replied, "Please thank them, but our parents will probably stay at the hotel with the rest of the family. We have rooms together for them, in a suite. That way, they won't inconvenience anyone."

"Another time." Mary left.

Ann thought again: it was Mary who gave the family welcome. It hadn't been she who extended the family concern, but Mary. Ann hadn't even thought about accommodations for Clint's family. Why was that? Perhaps it was because Clint always seemed to have everything under control. Then, too, she didn't live at home, and her own house was its usual casual self. How did one invite the parents of one's love to a poorly kept house?

Ann went to the nurse who had acted as liaison to those people waiting for information. Ann asked, "What does one do with children who are five and seven?"

The nurse looked blank.

"I'm not used to children, and I'm going to take the Durbin children home with me for the evening. How should I cope?"

"A slow bath? Books? TV? Let them help you. Keep them busy. Make cookies? Sew doll clothes? Clay figures? Pitch and catch? What did you do at that age?" The nurse's eyes kept straying past Ann to where Clint talked to his brother.

Ann asked rather pointedly, "And what do you suggest?"

The nurse raised her eyebrows as her eyes came back to Ann. "My mother had us pick bouquets of flowers. After the first time, she limited us to only enough for a certain vase. She would have us scrub the front porch, barefoot, with a hose and a little broom. Water is always soothing. Don't let them get too excited. They've had enough disruption for quite a while. Keep things peaceful. They may quarrel. They may cry. Be kind."

"Thank you. I think I can cope now."

"You will. Ask your sister to help you. She's a manager." She smiled beyond Ann to Clint.

Somehow that straightened Ann's backbone in an odd way. She said again, "I believe I can handle it. Thank you."

But when the girls came to them, Ann's heart fell right down into her shoes. They were children. Most kids of five and seven were children, but Clint's nieces were so small. They were very solemn, wide eyed and still. Like mice. They watched Ann with suspicion and didn't want to go with her.

Clint squatted down and said, "Ann will take good care of you."

They looked at Ann, not believing their uncle for one minute.

Ann stretched her mouth into a smile and tried to appear confident. "I have a cat named Mac. And I have a fish pond in the backyard that you can wade in."

Clint gave her the most marvelous look of relief. It was as though he had doubted she was capable of taking the girls, and he was only sending them with her out of desperation. Didn't he have any faith in her at all? Well, neither did she.

# Nine

Mary had told Ann that all it took to be in control was to have the conviction she could succeed. If Ann could believe that, she should be able to accomplish anything. Simple. If it was really that easy, she could do it.

Since the children had been traveling to visit, they had their favorite things with them. Jan, who was seven, had a cloth doll with yarn hair her other grandmother had made for her; and Cathie, less secure at five, had a blanket, a worn rabbit, and a hat.

Although Ann was a casual housekeeper, she was startled to see the condition of those three things belonging to the younger girl. They were dirty. As they organized themselves and prepared to leave the hospital, Ann said brightly, "We'll wash those," which earned her a horrified stare from Cathie and frowns of censure from everyone else in the family. Ann was too ignorant to realize she was treading on sacred ground.

When they had said goodbye to the family and were walking to the elevator at the hospital, Clint began tactfully to instruct Ann, "Right now, Cathie is inseparable from her blanket, the rabbit and that hat."

Ann was being efficient and in control, so she smiled at Clint indulgently. "All kids have favorite things," proclaimed the recent expert. "Mine was a stuffed duck. I loved him until all the feathers wore off and he was bare." She smiled in a cheerful, sharing way to the girls who watched her stonily.

Clint made several other attempts to warn Ann, but she wasn't receptive to outside, male advice. In the parking lot, he put his nieces into the back seat of Ann's rather dusty car—it had been some time since he'd washed it for her—and he told the girls bracingly, "I'll be by for you about eight. You'll sleep with us at the hotel. Okay?" Then he said to Ann, "Would you give them supper?"

She replied in firm confidence, "No problem."

They waved as they left the parking lot, Ann with good cheer, the girls with their noses pressed against the back window as if they were being sent into exile. When Clint's form had diminished to a dot and they'd turned east and lost him entirely, the two little sisters slid down and sat on the back seat, holding hands and clutching their security paraphernalia.

Ann tried. She asked what they'd like for supper. She asked if they had favorite television shows. She asked if they liked cats. And she received no replies at all. She ran out of questions within about five blocks. They drove the rest of the several miles to her house in silence. Ann bit her lower lip and wondered what she'd gotten into. Apparently the two little girls wondered where they were going and what would happen to them.

Mac wasn't home. After four years of feeding that worthless cat, when Ann finally really needed him, he wasn't there. She silently requested a bolt of lightening to find him.

Not knowing what on earth to do with the children, Ann showed them around her house, acting like a hostess. Since they resisted moving ahead of her, she led them, and they followed slowly as if they expected the floor might open up or something might drop down on them from the ceiling.

She took them into her studio. They looked around solemnly, moving only their heads and eyes. She asked, "Have you ever seen an artist's studio before?" They shook their heads.

And outside, in the August heat, Jan and Cathie silently stared at her unusual backyard, as they held hands. They made no comment. Ann showed them the swings. She offered to push them in the board swing. They shook their heads.

She led them into her Mable-tidied kitchen and asked what they'd like to have for supper. They shrugged their shoulders. Inspired by the nurse's admonition to recall her own childhood, Ann made finger foods.

They watched as she made them each a tomato rose, a celery chrysanthemum, and a winding of potato and carrot in a swirl stick. She defrosted some puffs and made some delicious fillings.

The girls wouldn't touch any of it. They finally had peanut-butter and grape-jelly sandwiches. Ann was disgruntled.

After they'd finished eating, they left the cluttered kitchen and went outside into the hot, humid evening where Ann removed the grid over the pond. Companionably, she then took off her sandals and sat on the side of the pond with her feet in the water. The girls stood and watched her. She invited them to join her. They didn't respond.

Jan held her doll tightly in one hand, and Cathie's sweaty little hand with the other. Cathie held her filthy blanket and rabbit, and she wore that dirty hat. Ann surveyed her guests. So Cathie wouldn't let anyone wash those treasures? No problem. Ann would get them clean.

Ann asked Jan, "You're the older?"

Jan looked at her as if she weren't very bright, not being able to figure that one out by herself. "Yes."

Ah-ah! Conversation! Ann felt she'd made a wedge. "I have an older sister, Mary. She's always been very nice to me. She took care of me."

Jan studied Ann for some time as Ann lifted her feet from the pond to let the droplets drip from her heels. She put them back into the water. Jan said, "I take care of her."

Ann nodded in understanding. She'd gotten a whole sentence that time.

Without any indication of arriving, Mac was sitting across the pond as if he'd been there all along. Ann canceled the lightening bolt. "That's my cat, Mac."

Mac closed his eyes to conceal his humor at his slave calling him "hers."

"He looks mean."

"He's a pussycat," Ann assured Jan.

Insulted, Mac stood up, arched his back, bushed his tail and spat at his obnoxious slave.

"Why *Mac!* Shame on you! Come here this minute!" Foolish, foolish woman. No one commands a cat.

He gave her a lightening-bolt glance and sauntered away, with a telling switch of his tail.

The two children stood closer together. What little trust they'd had in Ann had vanished. They were alone with a silly woman and a dangerous cat.

But it was hot. In Indiana's humid August heat, their tightly held hands were wet with sweat, and the water looked delicious. Very gradually those two small beginnings-of-people eased closer to the pond's edge, finally sat down and reached to touch the water.

Casually, Ann called their attention to the fish. They watched in the silence as the fish teased them, coming out from the artfully arranged water grasses and darting back. Ann tried to catch one. And Cathie laughed, one tiny sound, quickly smothered.

Eventually the girls took off their shoes as the sun began to set and eight o'clock came closer.

"Your Uncle Clint will be here soon." Did her voice sound as relieved as she felt?

But the reminder released something in the girls. They would be going to the hotel, and they hadn't yet dipped their toes into the pond. If they were going to, they'd have to do it soon. They exchanged a look.

Ann felt she could do anything. She was so triumphant as they finally put their toes into the water. Then they actually kicked a nice little spray! And that was when Ann committed a mortal sin. She reached and plucked the three treasures from beside Cathie, and tossed them into the pond with the fish!

To Ann's shock, Cathie immediately had hysterics! And Jan was protectively *furious*! Ann couldn't believe such turmoil. Cathie flew at her and pummeled her with tiny, ineffective fists, Jan yelled accusingly, and then Cathie flung herself into the pond, floundering in the water trying to retrieve her precious possessions.

Ann scrambled, attempting to salvage the child, plus her things, and hold off Jan. Pandemonium! And quite shortly, as the bawling, dripping trio stood staring at each other and yelling at the tops of their lungs, there were batterings on the wooden gate!

Ann quickly put the grid over the pond and latched it in place, then went to the gate to see what *else* could be wrong. It was several neighbors, none of whom she'd ever met.

"What's going on here?" they demanded, looking beyond her at the two wet, pitiful, weeping children.

"I've never heard such a ruckus!" another neighbor accused. "What are you doing to those kids?"

So all three began to talk at once. Ann was definite. Jan gestured and tried to get past Ann as she pulled on Cathie, who was yelling bloody murder and clutching her sopping-wet treasures.

It took a while to sort it all out. One indignant woman told Ann, "I'd think you'd have known better."

"But they're dirty!"

"So? Look at this yard! I've never seen such a mess. Who are you to judge?"

Things went along in that vein.

Ann was defensive until she suddenly realized she hadn't harmed the child, she wasn't *that* guilty. Mary wasn't there to retrieve her from this mess; therefore she ought to take control. So she said firmly, "Now just a minute."

They all were quiet.

She'd sounded as if she knew what she was doing, and they'd listened! It was amazing, heady.

She said, "I'll handle this. Thank you for coming. I'm glad I have neighbors who are alert and who come to help."

Mollified, they gradually left. But one woman turned back at the gate and said, "Never wash security things."

And Ann was left alone with the two hostile children, the pond-soggy treasures, an absent cat, and no experience in how to continue. But it was then she realized that the children had been through a horrendous couple of days, and they had every right to be upset. They'd already been stretched quite far enough for two who were so young. She went toward them, and sniffling, they backed away. She squatted down, out of reach, and she held out a hand. "I'm sorry. I didn't really understand."

They looked at her for a long time. Then Cathie hiccuped and began to bawl louder then ever, but she ran to Ann and threw herself into Ann's arms, almost knocking her over. Jan started bawling in sympathy, and Ann joined them, crying, too, reaching out an arm to include Jan. They sprawled over into the weeds in a tangle of arms and legs. It was all a soggy mess.

Clint didn't get there until almost nine. No one came to his knock, so he used his key and went inside the silent little house. He found them in the bedroom. In a strange assortment of garments, they were all asleep in Ann's big bed. On either side of Ann was a sleeping child, and at the bottom of the bed was Mac, who raised his head to snub the intruder. Clint ignored the cat. He saw that Jan held her rag doll, while Cathie was wearing a pristine hat and clutching a clean blanket and a spotless rabbit. And there were tear-stains on everyone's cheeks except Mac's.

Clint looked on his love and his heart almost burst with his feelings for her. What on earth had happened? But they slept so soundly that he would have to wait until tomorrow to find out. Tomorrow. He wished he was in that bed, in Ann's arms. He needed her. Natalie was a whole lot worse. She might not make it. Reluctantly, Clint turned away to leave them sleeping and went back to the hospital.

In the morning, Clint called and asked if Ann could bring the kids. Sam thought they should see Natalie one more time. Ann ironed their washed clothes from yesterday's debacle, dressed them, and took them to the hospital. Everyone was very grim, but they smiled at the children and touched them with compassionate tenderness. That made them cling to Ann's hands. It was Clint and his brother Rick who took the children into their parents' cubicle.

Mrs. Burrows came to Ann and asked gently, "How in the world did you manage to get Cathie to give up her things to be washed? No one else has managed that! We're all impressed."

Ann replied, "Stupidity." Because they were dull with emotional exhaustion, too much coffee and not enough sleep, the others turned their heads and listened to this distracting conversation. "It's a long story," Ann told Clint's mother. "I didn't realize exactly what was involved. But my blundering was a blessing in disguise. After the fiasco, we've become friends."

"What happened?"

"It's too emotional for you now. I'll tell you another time, perhaps?"

"You're very sensitive."

"On occasion." Ann's smile was rueful.

"Clint tells us you're a remarkable artist."

"Thank you. I've brought a watercolor of him for you." She had anguished over it, not really wanting to give it up, but she had brought it with her. She took it from her bag and proffered it.

Mrs. Burrows unwrapped the picture, and they all gathered to see it. Mrs. Burrows recognized the love in the creation and smiled at the artist. "Thank you."

Just then the five-minute visit to Natalie and Sam was up, and the visitors returned to the waiting room. They had gone in so scared, but they came out with grins on their strained faces.

The parents asked, "What?"

Clint hugged Cathie, as she wiggled to be released, and he allowed her to go to Ann. He told them, "The kids said hello, then Cathie said, 'Ann washed Bunnie, Silky and Tricky.' *And Natalie heard and she smiled."*

The family laughed softly with the helplessness of seriously troubled people; and that brought tears.

Jan asked Ann, "What's the matter?"

Ann knew to keep any reply to a child as simple as possible. "Your mother smiled."

And in that atmosphere of worry, with those whose tight control of emotions had wavered, the two little girls crowded close to Ann. Jan asked her, "Will Mommy die?"

"Not if they can help it." Ann had blundered into the perfect reply.

Cathie leaned against Ann's knees, looking earnestly up into her face and questioned in the harsh whisper of little kids, "What's going to happen to us?"

Having been a coward until recently, Ann understood exactly. She replied, "Look at all the people here who love you. All of them will see to it that you're cared for. Don't worry."

Jan stated, "We'll stay with you."

"Fine. Any time you like."

"Forever."

How badly children needed security. They needed to know someone was in charge and knew what was going to happen. Ann smoothed Jan's hair and straightened Cathie's hat, which must be named Tricky? It amazed her that they looked on her as a shelter. Her! It was probably because the other adults were distracted and disturbed. Again she said to the girls, "Don't worry." How many times in her life had Mary told her that? And it worked. At least it did with an adult saying it to little kids, or a big sister saying it to a little sister.

Sam's sister was there. When had she arrived? She came to the children and asked, "Are you all right?" They backed against Ann and nodded. "I'm your daddy's sister. I'm your Aunt Lucy. I live in Montana. I saw you when you were very little." Then she said to Ann, "You're...?"

"Ann Forbes. A friend of Clint."

"Oh?"

But Clint came to them. He smiled down at Ann with possessive eyes as he told Lucy, "She's the woman I love. She just hasn't adjusted to it, yet. Want me to take you home, woman-I-love?"

She blushed. "I have the car. Should we stay?"

"The doctor was just in. He told us Natalie said Sam's name! And the poor guy is right next to her and can't talk, with his jaws wired shut and elaborately stitched face. But he still has her hand. This is monumental. Natalie's smile for the girls was her first conscious reaction to another person."

Ann realized then that there was a lighter feeling among the family who waited there. They were more optimistic. She smiled at Clint. He leaned and kissed her. Ann said goodbye to the others, Clint again walked with Ann and his nieces to the car, and waved as they drove away.

Mable was there to clean up the kitchen. She welcomed the girls offhandedly, and put them to work. They laughed and scrubbed and wiped. They weren't unfamiliar with household tasks; their mother had been teaching them. Ann did sketches of the busy little girls.

The three were cleaning the pond that evening when Mary and Dingus came by, met the kids, and caught up on all the news. Then Dingus rolled up his shirt sleeves and pant legs and helped with the pond. Dingus did that. Ann thought she wasn't the only one who was changing. So was Dingus. She smiled at him, and standing in the pond with his trouser legs rolled up, he returned a rather formal nod of acknowledgement.

She was struggling with her laughter when Clint came. He greeted them all, then he said, "I thought the pond was just cleaned not long ago. You're going to spoil those fish."

In her clean hat, Cathie told him earnestly, "We soaked Bunnie, Silky and Tricky in the fishes' water, and they were *so dirty* that we could've made the fishes *sick*!" She had absolved Ann of all responsibility in the cleaning of the treasures and made it sound like a joint enterprise!

Clint grinned at Ann. "I love you, woman-I-love."

"Natalie must be better?" Mary asked carefully.

"Yes. There's hope."

The girls questioned him, "Is Mommy all right?"

But his reply was then cautious, "So far. She's responded to some questions." He looked at the adults, then simplified his report for the girls, "They're pretty sure your mommy can hear them. And she knows it's your daddy who is holding her hand. She's said his name, and he felt her squeeze his hand."

Clint looked so tired. It was Wednesday by then. The accident had happened three days ago, and each day had been a week long. They brought a lounge chair over by the pool for Clint, and he took off his suit coat and tie, then his shoes and socks. But instead of lying in the lounge, he, too, helped with the pond, and they all got thoroughly wet. And they laughed.

They had supper at the table by the cleaned pond. The children were in another interesting variety of Ann's clothing, but Clint had to wear a towel as their clothes dried. Ann fed them a lobster bisque, with hard rolls and a salad. The children made no objection, but ate cautiously, moving their eyes as their tongues tasted. Then they smiled and had another helping.

The children had been seriously involved in the making of the rolls, and their products were obvious. Their Uncle Clint guessed who was the baker of which rolls and the girls loved it because he was very impressed and knew how to appreciate homemade rolls. While Mary and Ann talked, Dingus and the girls helped Clint clean up the kitchen. Mary and Dingus left soon after that.

Then, wearing their dry clothing that was only a little rumpled, Clint told the girls they were leaving.

"Where are we going?" They moved over by Ann.

"To spend the night at the hotel with your grandparents." And realizing that they really didn't want to be moved around, he added, "All the relatives will be there, and they would like to see you."

The little sisters looked at each other and balked. "We want to stay with Ann."

Clint promised, "You can come back in the morning. But this time you'll have a change of clothing. It seems to me that Ann can't keep you dry."

Ann began to sputter explanations and her tongue twisted so that Clint laughed.

And the girls laughed. They hugged Ann goodbye, coaxing her to come with them.

Clint told the little girls, "Ann has to stay with Mac." Then when he kissed Ann good-night, he whispered, "I'll be back as soon as possible."

She waved from the porch as they drove away, then went inside to change the sheets and bathe. She put on a long white sleeveless cotton wrapper that tied at the throat and buttoned down its length.

As she waited for Clint to return, she trailed into her studio and began a watercolor of the girls cleaning the pond. She was still at it when he got back.

He came inside the door and turned as he closed it. Two fingers held a cleaner's bag over his shoulder. She slid off her high stool and opened up her arms. The soft cotton caressed her body, revealing it. But he just looked at her with such a tender smile. She didn't quite know what to do.

He said, "I'm so tired."

"Come to bed."

"I'm worn-out."

"That's certainly understandable."

"I feel very odd. Tired. Restless. Vulnerable." Softly he added another word: "Mortal."

"Yes." She took the cleaner's bag from him and went down the hall to her room to hang it in her closet. "You'll stay the night?"

"Please."

Mac was on the bed, cleaning his toes with exquisite care.

"Could Mac sleep somewhere else?"

She smiled, picked up Mac and explained to the cat, "This is because you weren't here yesterday when I expected you to be and when you did show up, you were rude.''

Mac hung from her arms, appearing defenseless to whatever would come. Ann opened the mended screen and dropped the indignant cat out the window. Of all things, he hadn't expected that again.

She went back to Clint and tenderly began to undress him.

''I want you very badly, but I'd probably go to sleep in the middle of everything.''

''Maybe not.'' She carefully removed his tie and hung it over the closet doorknob.

''I've never been so tired.''

''We don't have to make love. It will be nice just to be together.'' She began to unbutton his shirt cuffs.

''You astonish me. The girls love you. No one can get strange kids so completely comfortable so fast. I've never seen it before.''

''We went through a cataclysm...and somehow we survived. I don't recommend doing it that way, but we made it. It brought us very close, but it could have destroyed our ever being friends.'' She undid his shirt buttons.

''What happened?''

''I'll tell you when we have more time. You need to sleep.'' She took his shirt off his shoulders, down his arms, and put it on a hanger, since it was clean.

''I gave this number to the hospital.''

''Fine.'' She knelt to undo his shoelaces, and he sat down on the bed as she removed his shoes and set them aside.

''Was it about Bunnie, Silky and Tricky and soaking in the pond?''

"Partly. Mostly." She peeled off his socks.

"They love you."

"I love them. I don't love very many people, but I love those two. She took his hand, tugged, and he stood. She began to unbuckle his belt.

"And me. You love me." It wasn't a question.

"You, most of all." She opened his zipper.

"I think . . . I just might be able to have a small, quick taste of you. Just to reassure myself you're . . . real." He'd almost said "alive." "You wouldn't mind?"

"In the morning." She slid his trousers off his hips and down his thighs.

"What's wrong with now?"

"You need to sleep." He balanced as she indicated which foot needed to be free so she could remove the pants.

"Aren't you wearing anything under that wrapper? It's a very virginal, tempting white but it's so thin that it's almost transparent."

"Ignore it." She reached up and slid her hands under his briefs and began to ease them down.

"I could see better if you took it off."

She smiled at him. "You're supposed to go to sleep."

He helped her to her feet. "Pretty soon now." He untied the throat cord of her wrapper and unbuttoned it quite slowly from top to bottom, kissing the skin as it was exposed. Since her breasts were full, he had to nudge them apart with his burrowing face in order to kiss between them. His breath was very hot on her cool skin.

Having completed unbuttoning her wrapper, he rose to his feet and pushed the cloth back from her shoulders and dropped it off her arms, letting it fall to the floor. She stood in the dimly lighted room, naked before him. Lovely.

His breath drew in sharply, and his arousal was demanding. His big hands pulled her to him. Her body, so sweetly rounded, was crushed against the hard, muscular wall of him, and he groaned.

She teased, "Well, perhaps just a small, quick taste?"

"Careful. It might well be very fast."

"I wouldn't mind."

"Are we back to that?"

"No, I've been wild for you. You've driven me mad, then you withhold the solution."

"Wild, huh?" He grinned at her quite wickedly. "How wild?"

She turned and tugged him toward the bed. He pretended resistance. She pulled, then got behind him and pushed.

In his courtroom voice he said, "I want it noted, for the record, that I did resist. I'm not easy, you know." He managed to fall to the bed on his back. She came down on top of him. And she made love to him.

He lay a tense, rigid victim, deliciously used by a voracious woman. He allowed her greedy hands and mouth the freedom of him, until he could stand it no longer. Then he turned her over, laid her flat, and took her on a wildly thrusting, marvelous ride to the moon and beyond.

# Ten

Clint fell into a deep sleep, but Ann lay awake for a long time. What was she getting into? She hadn't lied when she'd told Clint she loved him most of all. She did. How could she be a free and aloof woman if she loved him that much?

And then there were the children—how comfortable they were with her. Before this, she'd never wanted children. These two were charming. And they liked her. They obeyed her suggestions. How incredible.

What would it be like to have children? They didn't come prepackaged at five and seven, well behaved, and trained. They came in as raw material. They took time and energy and . . . a great deal of commitment. Like men. Men took commitment—at least a man like Clint did.

He wanted to marry her. Could she change her life that much? He certainly tempted her. She turned over on her side to watch him sleep. He yawned and moved his shoulders tiredly. She saw that he wakened, and she knew the instant he realized where he was. His head turned quickly toward her, and he saw she was awake. He smiled and moved to take her back into his arms, sighed in great contentment, and went back to sleep.

All of that in just minutes. How charming. He'd been so glad to see her there with him. Like the children, he too, had been through a horrendous several days. Her heart melted as she considered his concern for his sister, his love for his family, his partiality to her.

She had a very strong distaste for marriage. She liked her life as it was. If she moved in with Clint, she would have to change. He was neat; she was not. His condo was not to her taste; it was much too formal. But then, this house wouldn't suit Clint at all; it was much too casual. In either place, one of them would be uncomfortable.

If they continued as they were, could Clint be happy? He was very family oriented, possessive. She went to sleep thinking of all the times he'd shown his possessiveness of her—at the gallery, at dinners, with other people and . . . in bed.

His disturbed breathing wakened her. Her eyes popped open in alarm, and then she grinned to see him. He was propped on one elbow, gloriously naked, and he'd lifted back the sheet so that she was bare to his avid—and possessive—gaze.

"I wish I could carry you around like Bunnie or Silky or Tricky."

She considered that possibility and discarded it. "With a briefcase, it would probably be awkward."

With slow deliberation, he reached one big hand out to lay it on her shoulder, and he watched his hand as he smoothed it down her arm. "You're silky."

She choked. "Uh, Silky, to my knowledge, is a rather ratty scrap of a baby blanket." Then, with exquisite drollness she added, "However clean it is, for the moment."

He wasn't distracted. "Like satin." He slowly drew his pleasured hand back up her arm, and allowed it to linger as it went across her breasts. Then it followed the line of her, down into the curve of her waist and over her hip, where it paused for a leisurely swirl. "You're magic." His voice was husky and his breathing quickened.

She bit back a sassy reply and was silent for him. She watched his eyes as they went over her slowly, appreciating the loveliness of her form. He smiled a little and glanced up to her eyes. He leaned to her slowly and kissed her lips softly.

As she lay on her side, the weight of her upper breast pushed onto the lower one. He lifted the upper one and then allowed its weight to return. He caressed her, then leaned his hot mouth to her and suckled, his hand moving over her stomach and around her hip, as his fingers reached farther to explore.

She stretched, lifting her arms slowly, turning onto her back, making his busy mouth release that nipple and take up the other, closer one. She was sinuous in her deliciously languorous twisting, yawning, lying full length, lifting her knees, moving her shoulders, turning. She relished the stretchings, like a cat. And she purred in soft, contented sounds, exciting him further.

It was barely dawn; the clock said five-thirty. The chirping birds were busy. And so was Clint. There were the sounds of his breathing, the silky slithering of his stroking hand and his greedy suckling. His mouth released her breast with a pop and moved to her stomach. He had her attention.

His hands had begun to tremble, and his movements were stronger, his hands kneaded, squeezing and rubbing. His breath was scorching. Her own quickened and her movements were no longer lazy turnings. He lifted his head and his black-lashed, fiery blue eyes looked down into her dark ones. He wore the most triumphant smug grin. He positioned her, thrust and whispered, "Frigid." Then he laughed as he stroked her.

She curled around him and followed his dance as wildly, as thrillingly, as passionately as he. Their breathing rasped, the bed creaked, their bodies slithered marvelously. And their passion carried them to the ultimate exquisite pause, which they met together and held furiously, so briefly, until they convulsed in a shattering climax, clinging together as they rode it out, to fall back, their bodies limp and unmoving.

They lay inert until he finally lifted onto his elbows to smile down at her. "And you expect me to leap out of bed and go to the office...now?"

She gave him a sinful smile. "I'm finished with you, for a while. You may run along."

He put his head down by hers and laughed almost painfully. "I love you, you wicked woman."

"I'm wicked? I was asleep! You had to go and reach out your hand and set me on fire!"

"Do I?" He lifted up again to watch her face. "Do I set you on fire?"

"You're a sexual pyromaniac. You must be, since we both know that I'm frigid."

"Now, I told you, don't make me laugh. I'm having trouble enough just breathing and pumping blood around. You would have made a great spy. If I could organize my thinking, I'd tell you any secret you wanted to know."

"In all the world, whom do you love?"

"A wild gypsy woman, whose body lies beneath mine at this very minute. Don't get me excited again. I have to get to the office, to be sure everything is all right. But I have to go by and see Natalie first. And Sam. Poor guy, he's a talker. Think of all the conversation he'll have stacked up by the time his face and jaw heal and he can speak again. It's mostly the stitches. People can talk with their jaws locked together." Very carefully, and groaning, he separated from Ann and flopped beside her. Then his hand groped until it found hers and he held it.

She rolled up on her elbow and leaned over him. "I'm glad you're such friends with your family. There are a lot of families that aren't friends."

In a calculated, sorrowful way, he told her, "I'm very lonely, living alone."

"Could you live here?"

He contemplated the feminine room. "Not enough closet space."

"I'm not sure I could live in your condo. It stifles me."

"We'll build a house after we're married."

She flopped back, sighing. "Ah, there's the stumbling block."

"Oh, by the way, my parents are coming by, later this morning."

"What?" she asked softly. Then stridently, "What did you say?"

She startled him. He replied a surprised, "Just that my parents will drop by later this morning. No big deal.

*"No big deal? My God! You should have told me right away!"* She furiously scrambled out of bed.

He was astonished. "What's the matter?"

"Matter!" She turned on him. "Your mother will think I'm a slob!"

"No, she won't. She likes you."

Ann asked the ceiling, "How can he be so *dense*?" Since it was unanswerable, she didn't actually expect a reply.

"Mother does, too, like you! She thinks the watercolor is brilliant!"

Ann folded her arms and said with great patience, "The watercolor is of *you*. She likes you, ergo she likes the watercolor of you."

With obvious patience, he explained, "Well, of course, she does. She's my mother. She hasn't any choice. She *has* to like me."

"I hadn't realized there are parts of your intelligence that are flawed." She wasn't sympathetic but nastily critical.

He was puzzled. "Why are you so upset?"

"Any woman wants to be approved by the mother of the man she loves. It's—"

He grinned widely. "You want her approval?" He sat up and folded his arms on his drawn up knees. "You're anxious?" He was delighted!

She gave him a cold, grim look that should have zapped him. She flung around and dug through drawers, abandoned them, went to the closet and shoved aside his garment bag unkindly. She tore her hair. She couldn't find anything suitable to wear. She looked at him in despair. He grinned back. She said frigidly, "I despise you."

He put back his head and laughed out loud.

She picked up a hairbrush and threw it deliberately wide, so that it crashed on the wall, missing everything precious. She stormed out of the room, came back, found her robe on the floor, put it on in jerks, and avoided even a glance in his direction. He was highly entertained and whistled as he went to shower.

She had a huge breakfast ready for him, and he emerged shaved and dressed perfectly. She avoided his kiss, but not the pleased pat he placed on her bottom. She pointedly had only tea. He ate with relish and sounds of savoring. She went to the shower.

She was standing there in the nice hot stream, in great melancholy, when he came into the steamy bath. He opened the window, turned off the water, dried her carefully, then held her head and kissed her thoroughly. He smiled into her bleak eyes. "If she doesn't love you, I'll draw and quarter her."

"I'll get the place neat. I promise. When will the girls get here?"

"I'm picking them up right away, taking them by the hospital and then coming here. It'll be about an hour and a half. Don't fret yourself, my love. I like you exactly as you are."

With her hair in damp snakes around her head, and her skin in goose bumps with the early-morning breeze from the window, she looked at him. She knew, right then, that he would be worth any effort.

He kissed her again, sighed, smiled at her and told her, "You make it very hard to leave you here. If you wink at me, I may quit my job."

"I'm not wearing my contact."

"Good thing. Behave."

And he left.

She changed the sheets and made the bedroom look as if it had never even been used. She stood in the doorway and looked at it with a stranger's eyes. It was completely impersonal, she told herself. But she saw it as it was—feminine drapery, seductive female colors, invitingly soft. She shut the door firmly, to close the wicked room from his mother's sight.

Would Mable get there in time to salvage the kitchen? It would be next. Any mother would want her son's...friend to have a neat kitchen. She scrubbed it up—meticulously. Then she changed into modest slacks with a shirt blouse. She twisted up her hair into a tidy knot, and she was ready.

Clint brought the girls. They erupted into the house as if it was Old Home Week, glad to see her and full of exuberance. "Mommy opened her *eyes*! She *saw* us. She's awake!"

And for a brief minute Ann forgot Mrs. Burrows's looming visit.

But then Clint asked her softly, his eyes tender, "Would you like me to come with my parents?"

She stiffened and jerked her head in little shakings. "No, no. No, no, no. Don't be silly. I can handle it."

"She's very nice."

"I know."

"If she's having a mid-life crisis and turns mean, dump her in the pond. I've learned from experience that ponds are very handy calmers."

"Oh, Clint..." She shook her head and gave him a watery smile.

Unfairly he ducked his head close to hers and said, "If you'd just realize it, Miss Forbes, you tend to like me a little."

Rather prissily she replied in a tiny whisper so that the kids couldn't hear, "Now and then. But only for sexual release."

He loved it. He laughed, with the kids jumping around, yelling, "What's so funny? Tell us, too!"

Clint told them, "Behave yourselves, now. Mind Ann. I'll be by at noon, for lunch?" He ended with a question, asking permission.

"Peanut butter and jelly sandwiches." Ann lifted her chin.

"You obviously have your finger on the pulse of the subteen world. I'll bring McDonald's for everyone. Okay, kids?"

They agreed jubilantly.

"Clint. When?"

He checked his watch. "It's still only eight-thirty-five. Not for a couple of hours yet."

She drew a bracing breath.

He put a big hand on her shoulder. "I've been out of the office for three days, another half-day won't mean a thing. I can go in at noon."

"No, of course not. You go on. We'll be fine."

"That's my girl. Woman." He kissed her, and on his way out the door, he fondly messed up Jan's hair and waggled Cathie's Tricky hat, which she clutched with both hands; but she laughed.

Because Ann took care of growing things, the big plants that Clint had had put in her studio thrived. She looked around the double rooms. They weren't too bad. The plants made it more cohesive. She would simply tidy it up. Her equipment wasn't sloppy; they were the tools for her work. It was just that there were so many different ones. And the stacks of drawings and paintings did get out of hand.

They began.

The children were earnest help. They looked at and sorted through the drawings, spreading them around, and exclaimed or were puzzled. It became very involved.

The ring of the doorbell was startling, and Ann jerked her head up in shock. It had suddenly become ten-thirty, and Clint's mother was there? What had happened to the time?

She looked at the girls. They weren't as neat as when they came—and neither was she. With dread, she got up and went to the door, followed by the girls.

It was the Burrows family—most of them. Ann stretched her mouth into a smile and stepped back for them to enter. Like everyone, they were snagged by the Chinese screen.

She heard his voice. Clint was there. They finally came into the studio, all talking, the children's voices mixed in with the adults'. Ann could have died. The studio was worse than ever. She watched sadly for Clint. He finally came around the screen and smiled at her, then glanced around. "Been busy."

"We were clearing things up," she explained sadly. "But we came across the drawings to illustrate a book, and I told them the story." Her gaze clung to Clint.

His relatives were looking around, picking up drawings, listening to the children explaining about them, and smiling. Ann watched anxiously. Even Sam's sister, Lucy, was there. She, too, poked around. There was an older woman Ann had never seen before. And Mr. Burrows studied the pictures on the walls, especially the large watercolor Ann had done of Clint that one time. There were nods and smiles. Were their smiles genuine? Or just polite?

Then Ann saw that one of the girls had left the bedroom door open and anyone could see into the seductive room. Ann was exposed as a fallen woman. This was her lair. Mrs. Burrows would snatch her son out of her clutches; Ann knew it.

Was she such a pansy to just...quit? Wasn't he worth fighting for? Didn't she love him? She looked at Clint and her musings from the night before expanded to include just how important he was to her, how very much she really loved him. Very much.

If she was positive, she could be in control, and she could do anything she set her mind to do. She said, "I'm so glad you could all come, especially since it means Natalie and Sam are better. They're fortunate to have you all there, giving them strength."

"And Clint is fortunate to have you." His mother smiled at her. "I've brought an old friend. She used to

work for the publishing house where you did some il-
lustrations. She remembers you very well, and she was
so pleased to hear we knew you that she asked to come
along. Do you mind?''

And Ann looked at the stranger. "No, not at all.
I'm delighted."

"Ann, this is Mildred Henshaw."

"Call me Millie. I'm an admirer of yours. How
marvelous to see your studio. Do you mind if I look
around?''

"Not at all."

They eventually drifted outside into the yard, and
there were no gasps of dismay at the sight of the un-
fretted yard. Her guests and the children strolled
around, observing the mixture of plants, sat in the
swings and inspected the fish. They all relaxed. Clint
went for McDonald's hamburgers, and they had lunch
at the table outside. It was very pleasant, and Clint's
family was extremely kind to Ann. Very welcoming to
her.

Lucy came to Ann and said in her straightforward
way, "I wanted to take the children back to Montana
with me until Sam and Natalie can cope again. It's
going to be a while before Natalie can handle the kids.
But Clint said you and he could manage. The kids
would be close by to visit the hospital and then they
can stay with you until they can go back home. I really
didn't think an artist was stable enough to handle all
that, but now I can see the kids would be happier with
you. Any kid would like living here."

Those statements did surprise Ann. Clint had committed her? Good heavens, but he was taking a lot for

granted! How dare he decide her life! What the hell was he trying to do to her? She shot him a cool look as she said, "It's too bad you live so far away. It was terrific of you to come to them. You must love them very much. Do you have children?"

"No. I work. But I could get a month's leave. I would have liked to help. But with you here, they don't need me."

Ann heard not only the words that Sam's sister spoke, but the wistfulness. "Would you like to stay here awhile? Before you go back? You'd have to share the bedroom, but we could put up another bed or two in there. The girls can stay, too, and you can get better acquainted with them."

Lucy brightened. "For a couple of days? I would love it."

How lonely Lucy was. It was then Ann knew that if she didn't take this chance with Clint, she, too, would be lonely for the rest of her life. Lonely for him. No matter how many people were around her, it was Clint who filled her life. She turned her head and looked for him. He was watching her. He was rested. He was confident. He was here. She smiled at him. He gave her a slow wink and held it that way. She laughed.

"What a nice laugh you have." Mr. Burrows had come up beside her as Lucy moved away. "Clint is a lucky man."

"A very positive one."

Mr. Burrows chuckled. "Has he told you that you're going to marry him?"

"Yes. But I haven't yet given my reply."

"Will you?"

She smiled at the pushy father of her arrogant lover. "Probably."

"He is assuming you will. You should hear his plans for you. I wouldn't wonder if he carried you off, if you should be so rash and uncooperative as to refuse him."

Again she said, "Probably." Her eyes danced.

"It'll be our pleasure to have you as one of us. Your parents are very kind. We were with them for a while last night. They came to the hotel, and we had a nice visit."

"Really?" Ann was surprised and very touched. They'd done that for her? Mary must have arranged it. Bless Mary.

Clint came to her. "I really have to go to the office. Walk me to my car?"

As they went through the gate, she said, "I understand I've volunteered to help out with the girls until Natalie and Sam recover."

He nodded rather absently, as if he already knew that and it was old news.

"You might have mentioned it to me."

"Don't you want to?" He looked startled.

"Of course, that's not—"

"Then what's the problem?"

"It's just that—"

"Are you peeved with me? I knew you wouldn't mind. You're part of the family."

She corrected, "The extended family. Lucy is staying here with the girls and me for several days."

"*Here?* How? There's just our bed."

"We're going to bring in two others for us, and the girls are going to sleep in the big bed."

He eyed her. "Is this revenge for not asking first?"

"Heavens. Why should I do that?"

"I don't like this setup, at all. We'll have to figure something out."

She leaned against Clint. "Lucy is lonely. She wants to know Sam's children better."

"They can have the condo, and we'll stay here."

"They'd all know we were sleeping together!" she protested.

"Well." He sighed in resignation. "Then the only thing to do is get married. Everybody is here, anyway, so why waste the opportunity? Think of the money saved in travel expenses if they had to come back next month!"

So Ann found herself married again, two days later. Sharon catered. Mary was maid of honor, Rick best man, and everyone had a marvelous time. Lucy said it was just a good thing she was there to keep the kids during the honeymoon.

Of course, the kids wanted to go along with Uncle Clint and their new Aunt Ann, and they couldn't understand why they couldn't. But they did get to stay in Aunt Ann's house with Aunt Lucy. And they had the pond, Mac, and eight tons of sand, which had been delivered the day before the wedding. A section of the fence had been temporarily removed and then replaced after the truck had dumped the sand.

Mac thought he'd made cat heaven.

So it was just the two of them on the honeymoon, after all. They went to St. Louis to see to Sam's and Natalie's house, to check on their mail and arrange

yard care, until the two could return. And the honey-
mooners used the house themselves for several days.

Lying in bed in the big, silent house, Ann told Clint,
"I can't believe I'm married to you."

"Did you expect me to live in sin for the rest of my
life?" His idle finger drew circles on her bare body.

"I'm not orderly." She made it a firm statement of
fact.

"I know."

She gave him a rather indignant look, but she felt
the need to add, "I'm really a little . . . arrogant."

He agreed. "Yes."

Her lips tightened, but she said the worst of it, "I'm
a loner."

He laughed.

She rose, annoyed, but he only indicated that she
wasn't in any way alone. He was undeniably with her.
She was part of a pair.

She ground it in: "We are very different."

"I must agree." He raised himself up, laying her
flat, in order to lean over her. His voice husky, he explained, "We are very different." And his hand went
over her "different" body.

She asked, "If you realized we were unsuited, why
did you say you loved me?"

"I do."

"Why?"

"You're more than those things that you say you
are. You're committed, responsible, humorous, kind.
And you love children—and me."

"You told me I'm a fabulous lover."

He said in absentminded instruction, "That's not a
character trait, that's a skill."

"Do you really think this frigid woman is skilled at making love?"

"I'm teaching her," he replied placidly.

"Don't touch me there, I'm trying to have a serious conversation. We're married. I'm not quite sure how this all happened so fast. I'm not at all sure this is going to work out."

"We'll manage. We have the basics in common."

"What basics?"

He kissed her long and marvelously, moving hungry hands and tongue. She gasped and sighed and moaned. He smiled.

Grasping one more time for coherence, she asked, "Are you sure this is the smart thing to do?"

"Yes."

"But Clint, what about all the differences?"

"We'll work everything out. Stick with me. We can do anything—together." The last word was said with soft, intense conviction.

Then he showed her some things they had in common.

\* \* \* \* \*

# SILHOUETTE™
## *Desire*™

# COMING NEXT MONTH

**#553 HEAT WAVE—Jennifer Greene**
Kat Bryant had always been cool to neighbor Mick Larson, but when she was forced to confront him about neglecting his motherless daughters sparks flew and the neighborhood really heated up!

**#554 PRIVATE PRACTICE—Leslie Davis Guccione**
Another Branigan-O'Connor union? According to Matthew Branigan and Bridget O'Connor—never! But when Bridget caught a glimpse of Matt's bedside manner, her knees got weak and her temperature started rising....

**#555 MATCHMAKER, MATCHMAKER—Donna Carlisle**
Old-fashioned chauvinist Shane Bartlett needed a wife and it was Cassie's job to find him one—an impossible task! But the search was surprisingly easy. These two opposites were the perfect match.

**#556 MONTANA MAN—Jessica Barkley**
He thought she was a spoiled socialite. She thought he was a jerk. Could Montana man Brock Jacoby ever tame a frisky filly like Jamaica McKenzie?

**#557 THE PASSIONATE ACCOUNTANT—Sally Goldenbaum**
Accountant Jane Barnett didn't like things she couldn't control—things like relationships—but Max Harris was proof that an emotional investment could yield a high return in love and happiness!

**#558 RULE BREAKER—Barbara Boswell**
Women never said no to rebel blue blood Rand Marshall, March's *Man of the Month*—but Jamie Saraceni did. One rejection from her and this rule breaker's bachelor days were numbered.

# AVAILABLE NOW:

**#547 DARING MOVES**
Linda Lael Miller

**#548 CONTACT**
Lass Small

**#549 RUBY FIRE**
Celeste Hamilton

**#550 LOCK, STOCK AND BARREL**
Cathryn Clare

**#551 HEARTBREAK HOTEL**
Jackie Merritt

**#552 A LOVING SPIRIT**
Annette Broadrick

You'll flip . . . your pages won't!
Read paperbacks *hands-free* with

# Book Mate · I

**The perfect "mate" for all your romance paperbacks**

**Traveling • Vacationing • At Work • In Bed • Studying • Cooking • Eating**

Perfect size for all standard paperbacks, this wonderful invention makes reading a pure pleasure! Ingenious design holds paperback books OPEN and FLAT so even wind can't ruffle pages — leaves your hands free to do other things. Reinforced, wipe-clean vinyl-covered holder flexes to let you turn pages without undoing the strap . . . supports paperbacks so well, they have the strength of hardcovers!

SEE-THROUGH STRAP

Reinforced back stays flat

Pages turn WITHOUT opening the strap

Built in bookmark

BOOK MARK

BACK COVER HOLDING STRIP

10 x 7¼ opened
Snaps closed for easy carrying, too

Available now. Send your name, address, and zip code, along with a check or money order for just $5.95 + .75¢ for postage & handling (for a total of $6.70) payable to Reader Service to:

Reader Service
Bookmate Offer
901 Fuhrmann Blvd.
P.O. Box 1396
Buffalo, N.Y. 14269-1396

Offer not available in Canada
*New York and Iowa residents add appropriate sales tax.

BM-G

# SILHOUETTE DESIRE™

### presents

# AUNT EUGENIA'S TREASURES
## by CELESTE HAMILTON

Liz, Cassandra and Maggie are the honored recipients of Aunt Eugenia's heirloom jewels...but Eugenia knows the real prizes are the young women themselves. Read about Aunt Eugenia's quest to find them everlasting love. Each book shines on its own, but together, they're priceless!

### Available in December:
### THE DIAMOND'S SPARKLE (SD #537)

Altruistic Liz Patterson wants nothing to do with Nathan Hollister, but as the fast-lane PR man tells Liz, love is something he's willing to take *very* slowly.

### Available in February:
### RUBY FIRE (SD #549)

Impulsive Cassandra Martin returns from her travels... ready to rekindle the flame with the man she never forgot, Daniel O'Grady.

### Available in April:
### THE HIDDEN PEARL (SD #561)

Cautious Maggie O'Grady comes out of her shell...and glows in the precious warmth of love when brazen Jonah Pendleton moves in next door.

Look for these titles wherever Silhouette books are sold, or purchase your copy by sending your name, address and zip or postal code, along with a check or money order for $2.50 for each book ordered, plus 75¢ postage and handling, payable to Silhouette Reader Service to:

| In U.S.A. | In Canada |
|---|---|
| 901 Fuhrmann Blvd. | P.O. Box 609 |
| P.O. Box 1396 | Fort Erie, Ontario |
| Buffalo, NY 14269-1396 | L2A 5X3 |

Please specify book title(s) with your order.

SD-AET-1R

**At long last, the books you've been waiting for
by one of America's top romance authors!**

Ten years ago Diana Palmer published her very first
romances. Powerful and dramatic, these gripping tales
of love are everything you have come to expect from
Diana Palmer.

In March, some of these titles will be available again in
**DIANA PALMER DUETS**—a special three-book collec-
tion. Each book will have two wonderful stories plus an
introduction by the author. You won't want to miss them!

**Book 1**
**SWEET ENEMY**
**LOVE ON TRIAL**

**Book 2**
**STORM OVER THE LAKE**
**TO LOVE AND CHERISH**

**Book 3**
**IF WINTER COMES**
**NOW AND FOREVER**

*Silhouette Books*®